A LLAMA FOR THE COWBOY
ELK MOUNTAIN RANCH BOOK ONE

RUTH PENDLETON

Copyright © 2022 by Ruth Pendleton

All rights reserved.

No part of this book may be reproduced in any form or by any electronic or mechanical means, including information storage and retrieval systems, without written permission from the author, except for the use of brief quotations in a book review.

Cover design: Daniel at thebookbrander.com

v.3

For my sunflower boy

CONTENTS

Chapter 1	1
Chapter 2	15
Chapter 3	30
Chapter 4	40
Chapter 5	50
Chapter 6	61
Chapter 7	70
Chapter 8	81
Chapter 9	91
Chapter 10	100
Chapter 11	112
Chapter 12	123
Chapter 13	134
Chapter 14	147
Chapter 15	159
Chapter 16	170
Chapter 17	180
Chapter 18	190
Chapter 19	201
Chapter 20	211
Chapter 21	220
Chapter 22	229
Epilogue - Three months later	239
Also by Ruth Pendleton	245

CHAPTER 1

The rain pounding outside didn't bother Porter Matthews, but the flood of water pooling at the base of the window well? That problem made his stomach churn. The water was seeping through the sides of the window, forming a small waterfall to the basement carpet. If he didn't take care of the flood properly, he'd have rotted baseboards a few months down the line.

Porter filled his arms with a stack of towels from the closet and grabbed the mop bucket before he stomped down to the basement. Wherever the flood was coming from, it was soaking through the carpet at an alarming pace.

He was sopping up the soaked carpet when the door slammed somewhere above him and a voice began shouting. Porter raced up the stairs, his stomach muscles clenching. The day really didn't need another emergency. His boots thudded on the wooden floor while he slid around the corner and ran into his brother, Reid.

"What's wrong?" Porter asked, straightening himself out. He leaned against the wall and let his heart slow to a steadier rhythm.

"You were the one that called me. Something about a flood?" Reid ran his hand through dark brown, wavy hair that matched Porter's. He cleared his throat and gave Porter a pointed look as a subtle reminder that Porter still had his cowboy hat on.

Porter plucked the hat off his head, grateful Mom Matthews wasn't anywhere nearby to start in with a lecture on proper cowboy etiquette.

Reid held his hand out for the hat which he hung on a hook behind him. "So, where's the problem?"

Porter jerked his head towards the stairs. "Basement. Near the pool table."

"I assume you already got the towels?"

"Yep."

"And the mop bucket?"

"Yes, Reid." Porter turned away so his brother wouldn't see his eye roll. Sometimes Porter wondered how he got to be the oldest when Reid seemed so much more on top of things.

"What about the fans?"

"Of course." The response was automatic, until he registered Reid's actual words. "Dang it. I haven't grabbed them yet. I was starting to clean up the mess but then I heard you bellowing. I'm pretty sure the Landons next door heard you too. Are you going to help?"

Reid fixed his steely green eyes on Porter. "It wasn't a bellow. But yes, I'll help. That's why I'm here." Reid headed towards the stairs. "I'm not surprised there's a flood. It's quite a storm out there."

"Yeah. I know we need the moisture, but couldn't the rain come in more manageable spurts?" Porter grabbed a fan from the hallway closet. He was going to have to search the storage barn for the other ones.

Reid shook his head. "Just a typical day on the ranch, lately."

Porter followed Reid down the stairs to assess the situation. In the brief time he had been talking to Reid, the water had moved along the floor another few inches. There was definitely something more than a heavy rain problem going on.

"Hey Reid, you got things handled here? I think we might be dealing with a broken pipe situation."

Reid looked up from the pile of towels he was holding. "I've got it. Bree should be getting home from school any minute and she can come help."

"Thanks," Porter said. He grabbed his hat once he was upstairs, wondering why he had even bothered to take it off in the first place. He should have known that following the stream of water leading to the basement window wasn't going to end well.

Porter slipped his arms through a rain coat hanging on the coat rack near the front door. The sleeves were a little snug, which meant it was probably one of his younger brother's coats, but speed was of the essence right now. Every second it took for him to find the water source meant that much more flooding in the basement. He could be slightly uncomfortable for a few minutes.

The rain was blowing sideways against Porter's back when he found the source of the leak. Sure enough, one of the sprinkler heads was broken off, with water bubbling out in a small fountain. There were large tire tracks nearby that looked suspiciously like someone had been driving in circles too close to the yard. If Porter was right, the twins had been messing with the tractors again. They had only been home for spring break from college for two days, and they were already up to their normal mischief.

He jogged over to the sprinkler valve, shutting off the water at the source. At least that would stop the extra flooding from happening. All Porter needed now was a new section of piping and a sprinkler head to repair the problem.

When Porter went to the basement to give the report, his sister was working alongside Reid.

"Hi guys. I figured out where the source of the water was coming from. I was right about the broken pipe."

"Can you fix it?" Reid asked.

"Yep. I'll get to it later after I run my errands."

"You were planning on going out in this storm?" Reid asked.

"Well, the pigs aren't going to be too happy if they run out of food. I thought we had a couple of bags left but the mice got to them first." Porter uncurled an extension cord and plugged the fan in at a safe distance from the flood. "It was going to be a quick trip but it can wait."

Porter headed to the window to check that the water was really slowing down. At this point, it was a small trickle. He caught Bree laughing in the window's reflection.

"What's that for?" Porter asked.

"When have you ever been able to make a quick trip to the store?" Bree dropped a towel on the ground and stood on it, the towel becoming saturated almost instantly. Porter guessed she would have used finger quotes if her hands weren't full.

"She's got a point," Reid said.

"You both are the worst." Porter shoved the mop bucket over to his youngest sister so Bree could drop her soaked towels in it. "Now, if you've got things under control here, I'll be back with more fans."

Porter bounded up the stairs before he could hear any other snide remarks from his siblings. He tucked his chin to his chest, trying to avoid the rain while he ran towards the barn. Sure enough, the large fans he was looking for were tucked behind a few bins of Christmas decorations. After a quick minute of jostling things around, Porter ended up with a fan tucked under each arm and an extension cord wrapped over his shoulder to the opposite hip.

Reid looked up when Porter bounded down the stairs with the remaining fans. "Thanks for grabbing those. You can head out now, if you'd like."

"Yeah," Bree said. "We've got things handled here."

Porter stood back to assess the situation. The water had stopped coming through the window and there were only so many towels to pass around.

"If you're sure," Porter said.

Bree plopped another soaked towel on top of the growing mound. "We're sure. And Porter?"

"Yeah?"

"I'll be timing you to prove that I'm right. Have fun at the store."

Porter didn't need to be told twice. He grabbed his raincoat and a set of keys, heading outside to brave the rain. Water had soaked the ground, forming large mud puddles for Porter to navigate while he made his way to the truck. Repaving the driveway was on the to-do list for another day. He filed it alongside items like repairing the cupboard doors, fixing the squeaky swing, and repainting the shed. They were all items that could wait until one of the siblings had a free day or the load on Porter's shoulders eased up.

Porter turned the key in the ignition, pumping the gas pedal to coax the engine to rev loudly to life. The truck had seen Porter through his fair share of years, from his first date in high school with the gorgeous Cassidy to the day he asked her to be his wife. They had driven it to the hospital when she went into labor with their first child, and a heartbroken Porter had driven it home alone after Cassidy and the baby passed away from a rare complication.

That had been eight years ago, but Porter couldn't bring himself to trade the truck in for something better. It was a piece of his old life that he wasn't quite able to let go. Porter could count on his fingers the ways his plans had gone awry. Widower at the age of twenty-five? Check. Losing his dad two years later when he was twenty-seven?

Double check. Taking over as head of an eight hundred acre ranch? Triple check. Life didn't exactly play fair with anyone, but his old truck had never let him down.

Mom Matthews had encouraged Porter to get out in the dating world shortly after the funeral, but how could he when he was stepping into his dad's shoes to take over the ranch? He wasn't going to leave his grieving mom and heart-broken siblings while he played on the town. Real men stuck to their responsibilities no matter how hard it got.

The truth was, his own heart had been too tender to think about dating anyway. He had married and lost his best friend. It was going to be impossible to find someone to fill her place in his heart. Besides, he didn't want to hear the rumors that would fly around the small Utah town if he started to date again, or deal with the helpful matchmakers.

Now that he was thirty-three, he liked to think he had outgrown the gossip mill. No one had tried to set him up for over a year. Maybe they were finally accepting his choice to be single.

The truck engine was making a noise somewhere between a purr and a growl when Porter backed out of the driveway. He shifted into gear and drove down the steep hill that led to the main road. By the time he was nearing the bottom of the hill, the rain had picked up so it was blowing sideways in sheets. The old wipers struggled to keep up with the deluge. Swishing back and forth, they did little to clear the windshield.

Porter discovered that if he shifted in his seat so that he

was hunched over, there was one patch of the window that the wipers were keeping decently clear. He was squinting through the gap when the truck thumped over something huge and then lurched to the side, sliding a couple of feet until it skidded to a stop, nose down in a ditch. Porter's body followed the momentum, his seatbelt tightening against the force.

The rain was pounding heavily on the roof of the truck when Porter turned the engine off. No point in wasting good gas when he was clearly going nowhere. He clenched the steering wheel, debating between saying a prayer of gratitude that the truck didn't flip or cursing the heavens for his bad luck. He glanced towards the heavens, and then bowed his head to say a quick prayer, thanking the Lord that he was okay.

When he pulled out his phone, his heart was beating fast but he felt calm. Reid and Bree were busy with the flood, but hopefully his brother Thomas would be able to come pick him up. The phone rang a number of times before going to voicemail. Porter left a brief message and then he tapped the screen to call Thomas again.

The phone beeped with a low-battery warning once and then the screen went blank. Maybe Bree was right when she told him he needed to upgrade his phone because this one clearly couldn't hold a charge. He reached for his charging cord, but someone had taken it out of the truck. The phone was useless now.

Porter gritted his teeth together. He was going to have to brave the storm if he wanted to get to the feed store any time soon. With the truck leaning at an angle, opening the door was a little more difficult than usual. Porter pushed against the frame, propping the door open with one booted foot while he reached for his wallet. He tucked the keys into his pocket and jumped out, hunching his shoulders against the cold rain.

Things didn't look good for the truck. The nose was at a definite angle in the ditch, raising the back tires a good foot off the ground. Porter circled the truck, looking for the source of the problem. As he expected, the front tire was completely blown, the rim almost completely stripped bald.

Porter walked over to the hill and looked up to see if he could find the culprit. A jagged piece of metal had gotten unearthed in the rain. The tire stood no chance against it. Porter jogged up the hill. Then he leaned down and began to tug, trying to remove the metal without cutting his hands. If he left it alone, the chances were that another person would lose a tire as well. He found a stick to help him pry the piece out.

The rain had eased up by the time he was finished moving the metal. It had taken a little bit of work to unearth it completely, but Porter felt like he was doing something useful with his time. He threw the metal piece in the back of his truck. It was an odd shape, but it looked like something his brother Finn might like to use in one of his garden sculptures. The twins were a handful, but they had good hobbies that usually kept them out of trouble.

Porter wiped his hands on his jeans to remove the excess mud before he leaned against his truck, weighing his options. He was far enough away from the house that it wouldn't make sense to walk back, but he was too far from the store to have that be a logical destination either. If he walked along the main road towards town, someone would eventually notice he was missing. With a dead phone and no one in sight, Porter had to trust that his brother would hear the message and come to help.

By the time Porter was ready to go, the sun was shining through branches that dripped with rain. He shrugged out of the rain coat, tossing it in the back of the truck. If the rain came back, Porter was going to regret his decision to leave it behind. It was a risk he was willing to take.

Porter held his head up high and walked along the road, trying to enjoy the scenery even though his jeans were soaked and his hands were muddy. It was an unseasonably warm spring, and although the ample amounts of rain over the past couple of weeks had been a beast to work in, the trees were loving it. The buds were opening into vibrant green leaves. In another month, everything would be covered in full foliage. Porter hummed while he walked, trying to let his mind sink into the moment instead of imagining what was happening at home.

Before too long, Bree would make some snide remark about being right that Porter was taking forever. Reid would brush her off. Then, as time went on, he'd begin to worry. He'd send Thomas to go rescue their brother, and all would be well. At least, that's what Porter told himself. He glanced down at his phone, but the battery wasn't miraculously charging any better than it had been the last time he checked.

He was walking down a narrow part of the road when

the hair on the back of his neck began to raise. A quick glance of his surroundings told him that he was alone, yet he couldn't shake the sense that someone was there. "Hello?" he asked, but the only answer was the wind dancing through the trees.

Pushing back the feeling of unease, Porter pulled his shoulders back and began to whistle while he picked up his pace. As he did, a rustling noise off to his left caught his attention. He moved towards the sound, stopping abruptly when he came upon furry hindquarters sticking out from the brush.

Porter approached the animal, his brain trying to make sense of what he was seeing. The animal was too tall to be a sheep, but too fluffy to be a mule. If he knew his animals well, he was looking at the hindquarters of a llama who appeared to be trying to break through the thicket to get to the greenery on the other side of the fence. He began to cluck soothingly as he got closer, not wanting to scare the animal further. When he reached the thicket, he jumped the fence to see what he was facing.

Large brown eyes stared back at Porter. Porter held his hand out, letting the frightened creature sniff him. "Hi there, Sir," Porter said. He waited for the llama to pull away, but instead the llama leaned his head into Porter's hand. Porter began to gently rub the llama's ears while he examined the brush that held the animal tight.

"Well, you seem to have gotten yourself into a bit of a mess." Porter pulled the branches to try to dislodge the llama, but the llama began to thrash wildly in protest, getting more tangled in the process.

"Okay, okay. I need a new plan." He stepped back from the llama and stuffed his hands in his pockets, watching the creature with great interest. As far as he knew, no one in the area had llamas, so where did this guy come from? Once the llama calmed down, Porter moved forward and began to rub behind the animal's ears once more.

He was moving to scratch under the llama's chin when a feminine voice called out to him from the road. "Who are you and why are you on my property?"

Porter stepped away from the llama and walked past the thicket to see who was addressing him. Sitting atop a brown and white spotted mare was a beautiful woman with dirty-blonde braids hanging just past her shoulders. She was wearing a pale brown cowboy hat, denim jeans, and boots that looked like they meant business. Stern blue eyes studied him with a look that said she expected the truth.

"Porter Matthews, and he started it," Porter said, pointing to the llama.

The woman straightened up in the saddle, her eyebrows raised. "My llama made you trespass?"

"Well, kind of. He was stuck and I was trying to help." Porter waited for a thank you, or even a smile from the woman but her face was impassive. "That's what we do around here. Help, I mean."

"Huh," she said, the word coming out as a cross between an accusation and a sigh. "It doesn't look like you did much to help."

"True. I'll admit I don't have a lot of experience wrangling llamas. And I don't have any rope with me to tie him to the fence, although he seems to have done a pretty good job at getting himself caught." Porter was rambling, which was not something he usually did. It was time to close his mouth and let the woman talk.

"So, what are you doing here again? Are you lost?"

Porter tilted his head back to meet the woman's accusing stare. "No. I'm just waiting for my brother to pick me up."

The woman's eyes went wide for a moment, and then she puckered her lips into a cross between a grimace and a smile. "Uh huh. And you magically appeared on this road? How did you get here?"

"Well, I had a little accident with my truck. It wasn't going to get me anywhere so I decided to walk."

She looked up the road and then back down the direction she had come.

"And where is this mystery truck? I didn't pass any vehicles on my way here."

"It's about a ten minute walk back that way. Just pass the turn off to Old Ranch Road."

She reached for an end of one of her braids, twisting it around her finger. The frown deepened. "Any injuries?"

The fact that she was asking about his safety meant there could be something soft beneath that scowl. Porter wanted to pull that side of her out.

"Nope. Well, except for my tire. That's a goner. The truck slid into a ditch. I'll have someone help tow it out when things have dried up a bit. My clothes had a bit of an argument with the mud but I think that's the worst of it." He was babbling again.

The woman nodded. "Okay. Anything I can do for you right now?"

He shook his head. "I'm good. One of the boys will come get me eventually." That was a nice, short answer.

"If you're sure." She raised her eyebrows, the doubt evident on her face.

"I'm sure."

"Alright then." The woman drummed her fingers on her leg. "Look. I know we've just met, but do you mind sitting with Stephen for a bit while I go get some rope?"

"Stephen?" Porter was struggling to follow her change of thought.

"The llama. He seems to like you well enough, and I really wasn't prepared for any runaways today."

Porter stepped back towards Stephen. "Not a problem. We're good hanging out here."

She nodded once and then turned her horse around. Porter watched the woman ride away, kicking himself that he hadn't at least asked her name. If he was thinking, he'd also have asked to use her cell phone to call someone. Now she was gone around the corner and it was too late. He was somehow stuck babysitting a llama for a perfect stranger. Hopefully the weather would hold for a while.

CHAPTER 2

*E*mily's mind swirled with questions as she rode away from the rugged, half-soaked stranger she had left with Stephen. His name tugged at the back of her mind, like there was something important she should know about him but she couldn't place it. She was guiding Maya down the driveway of her property when the pieces began to click into place. Porter Matthews. Old Ranch Road. There was a reason the name sounded familiar.

In her haste to make sure that Stephen was taken care of, Emily had failed to recognize that the cowboy trespassing on her property belonged to one of the most influential families in town. He may not be cowboy royalty, but a ranching family that was filled with handsome single men and women who weren't tied down? Their names swirled through the gossip circles quite frequently with Porter's being mentioned often.

Emily heard her first bit of gossip a couple of days after she moved to town. She was taking her trash can out to the curb when her nosy neighbor walked over and asked Emily if she was single. When Emily said yes, the woman smiled.

"How do you feel about cowboys, dear?"

The question was odd, but Emily kept her answer neutral. "I don't have an opinion, one way or the other. Why?"

"Well, you can't walk ten steps in this town without bumping into one. I'm just saying, if cowboys are your type, you may want to get to know the old ranchers." The neighbor trailed off, Emily walked back into her house, and that was that. She certainly wasn't interested in dating some old cowboy.

The second bit of information she picked up in the freezer aisle of the grocery store. A cluster of teenagers were hanging out between the ice cream sandwiches and the waffle cones, talking up a storm. Even though Emily tried to busy her mind with choosing her flavors, their words floated over to her. She caught all sorts of snippets about the three big ranching families in town. According to the young woman holding the basket, the Matthews family had the hottest men.

The other teenagers nodded in agreement, mentioning twins Finn and Wyatt. Then one of the young men brought up the baby sister, Bree. By this point, it was getting uncomfortable to eavesdrop. Emily cleared her throat and asked the teenagers to move to the side so she could grab her container of Rocky Road ice cream and be on her way.

At the time of the conversations, everything about the town was still new. It didn't really matter which family had the hottest men or where they lived. She hadn't come to

Elk Mountain looking for a relationship. She had come to open a llama therapy center.

That was why Emily was surprised at the heat rising on her face when she pulled Maya to a stop outside the stall. If the town gossip was correct, she had just asked the oldest brother of one of the biggest ranching families in town to babysit her llama. She grabbed the halter for Stephen, scissors, and a pair of pruning shears and climbed onto Maya's back, nudging her into a trot. Stranded or not, she was certain Porter had better things to do than watch a llama for her.

When she got back to the thicket where Stephen was stuck, the heat crept to her face again. Ten minutes earlier Porter was a perfect stranger. Now he was someone with a background that was much more interesting than that of a trespasser.

Porter looked up to greet her, and the smile that spread across his face sent flutters through her stomach. Even soaked in rainwater, everything, from his thick brown hair to his stubble covered jawline, made him the most attractive man she had seen in a long time. It didn't help that he had long eyelashes that perfectly framed his hazel eyes. The teens in the ice cream aisle were certainly on to something with their remarks about the Matthews family being hot.

She shook her head to clear the thoughts away. Looks didn't matter. Porter was in the right place at the right time to help. That was all.

"That was quick," Porter said.

"I told you that you were on my property. Just how big

do you think the place is?" Emily asked the question before registering that for Porter, it probably took much longer than five minutes to get from one side of his ranch to the other.

"You're right. I forgot that my crime was trespassing on your land."

"And your punishment was watching Stephen. How did he behave?"

Porter's low chuckle washed over Emily's body, relaxing the shoulders she didn't realize she was tensing. "Is he always this hungry? He spent the entire time with a mouth full of food, completely oblivious to the fact that his hind legs were stuck."

Emily dismounted from Maya and tied the reins to the fence. Then she walked towards Stephen, which drew her closer to the handsome cowboy.

"Well, llamas do like to graze." Emily climbed over the fence and slowly approached Stephen. She fastened the halter around his head while he chewed his bite, and then leaned forward so she could press her forehead to his.

"Do you want to tell me how you escaped, Mister?" Emily patted Stephen's nose and then turned her attention to the thicket surrounding his body.

"How do you plan to get him out?" Porter asked.

Emily held out the pruning shears. She studied the branches that were tangled in Stephen's wool and began to clip them, alternating between the regular scissors and the pruning shears depending on where he was stuck. He was going to need a haircut to hide some of the thin spots she was making.

Porter folded his arms across his chest. "Need any help?"

Emily straightened up and stepped back to assess her work. She prided herself on being able to finish tasks on her own, but the stuck llama was a little out of her depth. "Actually, yes. Can you clip any stray branches while I try to pull Stephen out?"

"I can handle that."

She handed Porter the clippers and took hold of the rope that was attached to the end of the halter. "Come on, buddy. Easy does it."

Stephen pulled against the halter, stubbornly digging his heels in as he refused to budge. Emily pinched the bridge of her nose, breathing deeply. She wasn't going to swear in front of Porter, but a few choice words were coming to mind. Did Stephen really have to act this way right now?

"Want to trade?" Porter asked.

Emily dug her own heels in. "I've got it." She put her body weight behind the rope and pulled Stephen's head around so it was facing her. "You've had your fun today, but now it's time to go home."

Stephen stared at her with his wide brown eyes. If it was a battle of wills, Emily would win. Keeping the pressure tight on the harness, she took a step back towards the road. Stephen reluctantly followed. After a few steps back and forth, Stephen gave up. He turned the rest of the way around and walked out of the bushes, shaking his head back and forth like he didn't have a care in the world.

"In all my years working the ranch, I have never seen

someone wrangle a llama." Porter had a grin on his face when Emily looked at him.

She smiled, in spite of her irritation with Stephen. "Well, I guess there's a first time for everything."

"Now that he is free, do you mind telling me your name?"

Emily weighed her options. It would be easy to give a fake name given how embarrassing the entire event was, but Porter deserved better than that. "I'm Emily Hutchings. Nice to meet you."

She held her hand out and Porter's hand enveloped hers. He had rough hands, calloused from years of working with heavy farm equipment. His handshake was firm, which made Emily smile. He wasn't being gentle on account of her being a woman.

"Nice to meet you, too." Porter tucked his thumbs in the front pockets of his jeans. "Now, what are you going to do with Stephen? Does he get a time out?"

Emily patted Stephen's back. "Not quite. Instead, he's coming with me to do the rounds."

"The rounds?" Porter raised an eyebrow.

"Yeah. Maya and I were out checking the fence to see if there was any damage after the storm. Given the fact that this guy got out, I'm guessing there are broken boards somewhere. I need to make sure none of the other llamas escaped."

That earned a snort from the cowboy. "Did you say other llamas? As in, more than just Stephen, here?"

"Yes." Emily resisted the urge to roll her eyes. "Doesn't everyone around here have a llama farm?"

"Not the people I know." Porter held his hand out.

"What?" Emily asked.

"If we're going to check the fences then I can take Stephen's rope."

Emily planted her hands on her hips. "Don't you have somewhere to be?"

"Truck problems, remember? Besides, my brother can pick me up from anywhere along this road."

Emily almost asked if he meant Finn or Wyatt but she bit her tongue. She wasn't supposed to know anything about his family.

"Alright." She handed the rope over. "If you're sure."

"I'm sure."

Emily grabbed Maya's reins and led her along the fence line, trying to ignore the cowboy walking beside her. When they rounded the corner, her stomach sank. A large tree had fallen during the storm and was now resting on a section of the fence, with broken boards visible between the branches. Part of the tree jutted just far enough into the road that it would be a hazard if cars were coming both directions at the same time.

Emily pulled Maya to a halt. "Do you mind if I check it out?" she asked, but Porter was already wrapping Stephen's rope around the fence and heading to the tree. No surprise there. It was fitting that the cowboy would want to help make sure everything was okay.

Up close, the tree looked much more manageable to deal with. The branches were long, but spaced apart enough that a saw would fit easily between them. She was leaning down to run her hand along one of the broken fence boards when she heard a loud crack.

Porter was standing on the opposite side of the wide tree. "Want to pass me those clippers?"

"Sure. Why?"

He looked her way, fixing his hazel eyes on her face. "These branches could scrape a car if it drives too close. I'd like to clip some of them back."

"Good call." Emily passed the pruning shears to Porter and pulled out her phone to take photos of the fallen tree for insurance purposes. If she happened to get Porter in a couple of the shots? That was purely a coincidence.

Before long, Emily could hear a trill that indicated she had company. She looked at the other side of the fence, smiling as three of her llamas approached to investigate the noise.

Porter was clipping the tip of a branch when he noticed their visitors. A huge grin broke across his face, his handsome eyes lighting up. "What is happening?" He gestured towards the llamas. "I'm guessing these are the guys you were worried about?"

Emily nodded. "Meet Bonnie, Cupid, and Wren."

Hearing their names, the llamas walked as close to the fence as they could get. Porter looked at Emily. "May I?"

"Sure. Just remember to let them sniff your hands first. They like to know who they are meeting."

Emily watched the cowboy hold his hand out to Cupid, and her stomach did a happy little flip. The llama seemed to like him.

"Who is this handsome guy?" Porter asked.

"That's Cupid. He's got a knack for calming down people in tense situations." He had managed to stop her parents from bickering long enough to hold a civil conversation when they were at one of their lowest points. Emily knew, at that moment, that Cupid was special.

Porter had moved on to Wren. She stretched her neck out so her cheek was near Porter's and he froze in place. "Did I do something wrong?" he whispered.

Emily walked to his side and reached out to rub Wren's head. "Wren likes you. This is how she says hello."

Porter leaned his head to the side and rested it against Wren's cheek. "Hello, Wren. I'm Porter."

Then he straightened up and held his hand out to Bonnie. Instead of coming to greet Porter, she hummed a trill chirp and backed up a few steps. Porter's face fell.

"I don't think she's a fan."

Emily leaned against the fence and coaxed the llama forward until she could pet her soft wool. "Bonnie can be a little shy at times, but if you give her a chance, she'll warm up to you." She straightened up and headed to the saddle bag, grabbing out a carrot for each of the animals. "This may help."

The butterflies in her stomach danced when Porter's hand brushed against hers to take a carrot. He held the carrot out and Bonnie trotted over to investigate. Porter waited for her to grasp the end before he let go. While she chewed, Porter looked at Emily, his eyebrows raised.

"Do you think I can say hi now?" he asked.

"I think so. She'll let you know if she's ready." Emily held her breath as Porter reached his hand out, willing her llama to behave, but she didn't need to worry. Bonnie leaned her head against Porter's hand, coaxing a giant grin from the cowboy.

Emily was enjoying watching the interaction, but she still had a lot more work to do. "Alright. Playtime is over. Are you ready to go?" she asked.

Porter nodded his head and walked over to grab Stephen's rope. Emily's heart raced against her will. There was something incredibly attractive about a man who was good with animals.

"Tell me more about the llamas," Porter said.

"What do you want to know?"

"I met the three of them. Do you have any others?"

Emily turned her head to look at Porter. "Are you actually interested or are you trying to be polite? Because I'm pretty sure I could talk your ear off once I get started."

Porter's body shook with laughter. "Aren't most people interested? I mean, you're in horse country here. Most of the ranches have the typical farm animals. We don't see a lot of llamas. I really do want to know more."

"Okay. I warned you." Emily took a breath. "I have five llamas right now plus Maya." She patted Maya's side. "I started raising llamas when I was a teenager. Stephen was my first pet."

"My handsome buddy Stephen, here?"

"Yep. I saved every dime for three years before I was able to buy him. My grandpa took me to his friend's house and they let me choose one of the babies. I was looking at a sweet little tan llama when Stephen trotted up, his dark brown wool sticking up in all directions. He had been rolling in some hay and he was a mess. I guess you could say it was love at first sight."

"I can see why. Where did the rest come from?"

"Well, llamas are social animals. I didn't realize that at the same time I bought Stephen, my grandpa was getting me a second llama as a present. The day we drove to pick up Stephen, Wembley was waiting with a bow around his neck."

"I didn't meet Wembley, did I?"

Emily loved that he was paying attention to their names. "Nope. He's probably checking out a different part of the property."

"Got it. What did your parents say when you came home with two large animals?" Porter was watching her as they walked, his hazel eyes bright with curiosity.

"I thought they were going to be so mad, but Grandpa had already cleared it with them. I was allowed to keep both llamas. That was all it took to cement my obsession with them."

Emily's happy mood talking to Porter fled when they turned the corner. A large section of fencing was down, with boards laying on the ground. Emily sighed. "I think we found where Stephen escaped. I'm so glad the others weren't with him."

It was definitely a problem that needed to be fixed. Emily was relieved she had trusted her gut when she felt like she should check the perimeter of the ranch. Her llamas were going to be safe even though that meant cutting her time short with Porter.

"I'd better head back and grab supplies to fix this mess."

Porter nodded. "Sounds good. I'll follow you."

It was surreal to have Porter walking a llama next to her. She had to make the most of the short time they had left. "I forgot to ask. Where were you headed before your truck slid off the road?"

Porter rubbed the side of his neck. "Would you believe it was a simple run to the feed store? Who knew that getting bags of food could be so destructive?"

Emily gestured towards the cloudy sky. "I blame the rain. It didn't exactly play nice today."

"That's for sure. We had a flood inside the house that rivaled the rain outside."

"Seriously?" She was surprised that he was so upbeat after the day he was having.

Porter turned to face Emily with a smirk. "Yeah. I can't really blame the flood on the storm, though. I'm blaming my twin brothers Finn and Wyatt. I'm pretty sure they broke a sprinkler head when they were messing around."

"How old are they?" According to the gossip mill, the twins were at college but Emily wasn't supposed to know that.

"They're nineteen and visiting for spring break. They've only been home for two days and are already up to their normal mischief."

"How on earth did anyone let you leave your house? What about the flood?"

"My brother and sister had it under control. Although, I may be in a little trouble when my siblings realize how long I'm taking." Porter shook his head. "It's my baby sister,

Bree, that's going to give me the most grief. She's sixteen but she thinks she owns the ranch."

Emily turned Maya's head towards the driveway. "My sister Kayla is like that but she's twenty-three. She hasn't outgrown the bossy phase yet."

Porter was nodding. "It figures. I guess most families have at least one person who wants to be in charge."

"For sure." Emily felt a pang that her time with Porter was coming to a close. His cheerful mood was refreshing to be around. "My truck is here. Do you want to borrow it so you can get to the store?"

Porter shook his head. "Thanks, but no. The water is already turned off at the house and my siblings are taking care of the flood. Your fence problem, on the other hand, isn't going to be okay if the llamas discover it. I think my time would be better spent here."

A surge of gratitude swirled through Emily. She was capable of fixing a downed fence, but it would go so much faster with Porter helping out. And if they had a chance to talk a bit more? Even better.

Porter held Stephen's rope up. "Want to trade? I can take Maya's saddle off and you can put this escape artist wherever he is supposed to go."

"That would be great." Emily snuck glances at Porter when he reached for the first buckle, but it was clear that he knew his way around horses. He looked incredibly good taking care of Maya.

They were heading to the shed when Porter's face fell. He turned to Emily and her heart sank. He was going to bail after all.

"I just remembered something. Do you have a phone charger I could use? I really should call home so they don't worry."

Relief flooded through Emily's body. He wasn't ditching her yet. "Of course. Right this way."

Emily took Porter to the small farm house that she was turning into the llama therapy center. She rummaged through a box of supplies until she found the universal charging cord that her dad had given her. Porter plugged his phone in with a grateful smile.

"You good, here?" Emily asked.

Porter nodded.

"I'm going to go load the truck with the boards we need."

"Alright. I'll meet you out there in a few minutes."

Emily was hefting boards into the back of the truck when she realized how comfortable Porter made her feel. Leaving a stranger alone in her office was not something she thought she'd ever do.

She was so lost in her thoughts that she jumped when Porter cleared his throat behind her.

"Things are squared away at home. Let's get this fence taken care of." He walked past the back of the truck, confusion filling his face. "That's a lot of boards."

Emily pointed to a stack leaning against the wall. "I want to load the rest of these as well. I'd rather have the extras on hand in case I find another downed section." She reached for a board, waving away Porter's attempts to help.

When the truck was loaded, she climbed into the cab. Porter slid into his seat and turned to face her with a grin that lit his eyes. Emily refused to let herself get distracted by his face. Otherwise, she was going to start giggling about the cute man like she was a teenager with her first crush.

There wasn't time for that. She had work to do.

CHAPTER 3

*P*orter wanted to pinch his arm to see if he was dreaming. A day that had started out with chaos was turning into an adventure. He was riding in a truck next to the intriguing Emily Hutchings, on his way to help repair a fence for her llama ranch. That wasn't something he could have imagined. Emily was beautiful, but she was also resourceful.

As they pulled out of the driveway, a snowy white llama ran up to the fence to watch them leave. "Let me guess. Wembley?" he asked.

"I figured you'd see him before too long. He doesn't miss out on much."

Porter watched the llama until they were around the corner. "I've met four of the llamas so far and seen Wembley. Do you think I could officially say hi to him? We could grab lunch some day and you could tell me more about your plans for the ranch." The words were out of his mouth before he registered that he had just asked Emily out on a date.

Her cheeks flushed with the faintest hint of pink. Clearly, she understood the question, but she didn't answer right away. Instead, she brought both hands up so they were clasping the steering wheel tightly. "It depends on how this job goes."

The answer wasn't a yes, but it wasn't an outright no, either. Porter leaned back in his seat and watched the trees flicker by. The trip to the downed fence was much faster by truck, which was good since the pressure in the cab was getting heavy. He breathed a small sigh of relief when Emily slowed the truck, pulling off to the side of the road.

Learning quickly, Porter only made the mistake of asking to help carry the boards once. Emily clearly wanted to do the job on her own. Instead, he matched her load for load until they had a stack of boards on the ground to choose from.

The rain had soaked the dirt, allowing a few of the posts to lean sideways. Emily shook her head. "We can prop these up so they will hold for now."

Porter helped Emily hammer the boards into the posts, crossing the top and bottom rungs so the llamas couldn't squeeze out.

Emily was so silent while she worked that Porter was afraid he had offended her. Talking to Emily had been easy when they were helping Stephen. Now he felt like a bumbling fool. He looked for any topic to land on, but nothing felt safe except for chatting about the llamas.

Scrambling to land on any other topic, Porter was

getting ready to make a comment about the weather when a truck slowed to a stop beside him.

"Hey, Port. Need a ride?" Thomas was leaning across the passenger's seat, watching him with an exasperated look that Porter knew well. He guessed Thomas had been in the middle of something important.

Porter glanced at Emily, who gave him a thumbs up. "I've got it from here," she said. "Thanks for your help."

Porter climbed into his brother's truck, the heavy weight of unfinished business following him. Thomas was pulling forward when Porter asked him to stop. He rolled down the window, feeling a surge of bravery.

"Hey, Emily?"

She looked up. "Yeah?"

"I was serious about taking you to lunch. How about it?"

Emily lowered the hammer to her side and leaned against the fence. Her face was a mask until the faintest smile began to dance around her lips. "Alright, cowboy. You proved your worth today. When do you want to go?"

There was no time for hesitation. "How about Wednesday at 1:15?"

"Don't be late," Emily said. Then she turned back to the fence.

Thomas waited until Porter's window was up before letting out a loud whoop that filled the cab.

"Hey, don't get too excited," Porter said. "It's just lunch."

"Yeah, but how long has it been since you've even thought about asking a woman out?"

Thomas had a point. He was two years younger than

Porter, but he was observant. Of all the siblings, it wasn't surprising that Thomas was keeping tabs on Porter's dating life.

"Look, she helped me out when I was stranded today. I'm just buying her lunch to say thank you. Speaking of rescuing, can we go pull the truck out? It's on the way home."

Thomas nodded. "Yeah, yeah. We'll get the truck." He glanced Porter's way and Porter knew he wasn't going to be able to evade any questions about Emily. Sure enough, Thomas began talking again.

"All I'm saying is that I saw the way you were watching that girl. Would it be the worst thing in the world to have someone to spend time with?"

Porter didn't have an answer to that. He watched the scenery flit by, waiting for the familiar pang in his heart to come at the thought of dating someone new, but for the first time in as long as he could remember, it was just the faintest of thuds. Maybe Thomas was right, and it was time to start thinking about opening his heart again.

The sun was casting long shadows on the road by the time Porter and Thomas got his truck out from the ditch and ready to roll. Thankfully, he had a spare to put on since the metal piece had shredded the tire around the rim.

Porter's stomach was growling something fierce when they finally got home. His quick trip to the store had taken a little over five hours and he had completely missed lunch.

Bree was waiting to pounce when he walked in. "I told you it would take forever."

Porter reached out to rub the top of Bree's head, laughing when she danced away. "This time it's not my fault. My truck slid into a ditch."

Thomas walked in the room, hanging his hat on a hook. "But the pretty girl you were fixing fences with wasn't anywhere near your broken truck."

Bree squealed and grabbed Porter's hands. "Details. Now."

Her eyes were so bright, Porter couldn't disappoint her. "There's not much to tell. My tire blew out, landing my truck in the ditch, and my phone died when I was trying to call for help. I started walking and Emily came to my rescue."

"Ooh, Emily. What is she like?" Bree rocked forward on the balls of her feet and Porter had to hide a smile. She'd been doing that whenever she got excited since she was old enough to walk.

He glanced over at Thomas, but Thomas wasn't going to spill the beans. In that moment, Porter felt a surge of gratitude that his brother wasn't a huge gossip. Porter wasn't sure of his own feelings about Emily. He definitely didn't need his brother filling in the blanks.

"Don't get too excited," Porter said. "She's just a nice woman I met who moved here recently." There was no need to mention how pretty she looked, hefting boards around with her sassy, independent streak. And the thought of her blue eyes that pierced through him didn't need to be mentioned either. "You'll never guess what kind of animals she raises."

Bree's face lit up. She rubbed her hands together. "Let's see. Rabbits?"

"Nope. They are a bit bigger than that."

Bree and Thomas followed Porter to the family room where they all plopped down on a large couch.

"Sheep?" Thomas asked. "I know there are a few sheep farms around here."

"Nope. But they are soft like sheep."

"Zebras?" Bree asked. "My friend Sunny was telling me about a family that has a zebra living on their ranch. They've helped rescue all sorts of wild pets."

Porter smiled. "That would be cool, but no, nothing so exotic." He was propping his boots up on the coffee table when his mom walked in and nudged them off.

"No shoes on the table. What are you guys talking about?" she asked.

Thomas cleared his throat but Bree was already on a roll. "We're trying to guess what kind of animal Porter's new girlfriend owns."

Mom's eyebrows shot up. She pushed a hand through her thick, black hair that was graying at the temples. "Girlfriend? I guess a lot has happened since I talked to you this morning." She sat on an armchair and clasped her hands on her lap. "Tell me more."

Porter reached over and grabbed a strand of Bree's curly, brown hair, giving it a gentle tug. "This one has an active imagination. I slid the truck into a ditch and a woman helped me out."

Her brow furrowed at the mention of the accident. "Are you okay?"

"Yes, Mom. The rain unearthed a piece of metal that blew my tire."

"And the truck?"

"We got it out," Thomas said. "The front is a little banged up but it drives fine."

"I'm so relieved. So, all that leaves now is this mystery woman's animals?" Mom fixed her eyes on Porter.

"Yes," Bree said. "And I was getting closer with my guesses, right?"

Porter could hear rustling in the kitchen. If he didn't end this conversation soon, the entire family would trickle in and join the guessing game. The last thing he needed was to be teased by all his siblings.

"Yes, you were getting closer. But now my stomach is grumbling and I want to go eat. She has a herd of llamas."

Bree brought her hands to her chest. "Oh my gosh. Llamas are the cutest. You're going to bring me with you to meet them next time you visit, right?"

Porter shook his head. "It's not like I have any regular visits scheduled with her."

"Except for the lunch date on Wednesday," Thomas said.

Porter lunged for his brother, growling when he squirmed out of the way. So much for not being a gossip. As luck would have it, Reid came into the room right when Porter grabbed Thomas and was placing him in a headlock.

"What did I miss this time?" Reid asked.

"He was late because he was busy finding a new girl-friend," Bree answered. She grinned at Porter. "I, personally, am ready to finally get another sister-in-law."

The room came to a standstill, with all eyes turning towards Bree. She blushed, the tips of her ears turning bright red. "I'm so sorry, Porter. I didn't mean it that way."

Porter let go of Thomas and straightened up, but before he could speak, Mom stood and shooed everyone from the room. "You're fine, Bree. Go find the twins and get washed up for dinner."

She reached for Porter's arm, holding him back while he tried to follow after his siblings. All it took was a slightly raised eyebrow for Porter to stay behind.

Mom placed her hand on his shoulder. "Port?"

He closed his eyes, taking a deep breath to clear his mind. There were emotions swirling through his body, but they didn't hurt as badly as normal. "I'm okay."

Mom smoothed her apron. "You say that a lot. Are you really?"

Porter held his sides, waiting, again, for the surge of emotion that usually lanced through his heart when he thought of Cassidy, but the stabbing was duller. "I don't know how to explain it. In the past, the thought of even talking to another woman had no appeal to me. I'm not looking for anyone. I had my happy story with Cassidy and little Claire, but after today, I am wondering if there might actually be more."

"You lost your spouse at such a young age. I forget that you aren't going to deal with it the same as I did when I lost your father. Sometimes I get so caught up in my own loss that I forget to check on your heart."

"I'm an adult. I can take care of my own heart." Porter gestured towards the kitchen. "It's not like I'm sixteen like Bree."

"True, but I'd like to think that all my kids will still want my advice, even when they are wise old humans at thirty-three."

Porter draped an arm across his mom's shoulders. "You're right. I do still need your advice. So, if you aren't too busy forgetting to check on me, what would you tell me?"

"I'd tell you that it's okay to follow your heart. I don't know all the mysterious workings of the Lord, but I do think that there are very few things that happen by accident."

"You're saying God pushed my truck off the road so I'd meet Emily?"

Mom's smile deepened the laugh lines around her eyes. "No. I'm not saying God pushed your truck off the road, or made the metal stick up, or anything like that. But I don't know how much of a coincidence it was that you were walking down the road at the exact right time for Emily to meet you."

Porter shrugged. "I don't know if I believe that."

Mom wrapped her arm around her son's waist, giving him a quick hug. "And you don't have to. All I'm saying is that if this Emily is making your heart want to be open again, I don't think there is anything wrong with exploring that. You don't have to marry the girl, but maybe she'll have something to offer you that you haven't wanted before."

There was a loud crash from the kitchen. Mom pushed the hair back from her face. "That's my cue."

Porter rested his hand on her arm. "Thanks, Mom. You've given me some things to think about."

He waited until she was out of the room before he sank to the couch. Why did everything have to be so complicated? When he was young, taking someone on a date was as simple as asking. Now every move seemed to carry so much weight. Did God really place Emily in his path? Would it be a betrayal to Cassidy if he took Emily out?

He closed his eyes and said a quick prayer. "Dear Lord, if it is thy will for me to open my heart again, please let me know."

The words hung in the air, but there was no answer. Porter was going to have to figure out the next steps on his own.

CHAPTER 4

*E*mily's stomach hadn't stopped dancing since she ran into Porter on the road. His kindness was unexpected. He had responsibilities of his own, yet he wanted to take the time to help her out. Him being incredibly handsome? That was an extra perk. If her neighbor asked her if she was into cowboys today, she may have a different answer than she had before. She wasn't into all cowboys, but Porter had certainly caught her eye.

Thanks, in part, to Porter, the rest of the fence repairs were pretty simple. A few nailed boards here and there, and Emily found herself back on the ranch with way too much time on her hands. She brushed down Maya, rearranged the horse tack on the wall, and ordered supplements for the llamas, but none of the tasks could counter the way her mind kept wandering back to a certain cowboy with a charming smile.

Emily threw down the shovel she was holding with a huff and went to the office. The building was old, but the walls were sturdy. The realtor helping Emily to find her property had been confused when Emily passed on parcels of land that were larger and in better shape, but Emily was looking for something that felt right. When she saw the ranch with an old house near the entrance, she knew it was the place.

Emily sat down at the folding table in the kitchen and powered up her computer. She crossed her fingers as the screen came to life. All she was waiting for was approval from the city and then she could open her llama therapy center when she was ready. It took only a second for Emily to scan her inbox to see that the city hadn't responded yet. Why was it taking so long to get a permit?

There wasn't anything else pressing to do on the ranch so Emily drove home. When she walked in the door, her phone began to ring. Emily threw her keys in the bowl by the front door and answered the video call. As her grandpa's nose filled the screen, Emily's tension ebbed away.

"Hi Grandpa," she said. "Remember that I can't see your handsome face if you hold the phone so close."

Grandpa Hutchings pulled the phone back so his balding head appeared. "How's my favorite granddaughter doing today?"

"You say that to all of us."

He winked. "But I mean it when I talk to you."

Emily grabbed her fuzzy blanket and sat on the couch. "Well, you're my favorite grandpa so I guess it works."

Her grandpa nodded. "Exactly. How's the ranch?"

"We had a huge storm that took out some of the fence

line, but the damage isn't too bad. I had a little help and got it taken care of."

"I'm glad you're making friends. Any news from the city?"

Emily pulled her legs up so she was sitting cross-legged on the couch. He wouldn't be so casual with the questioning if he knew that her helper was a man. "Still nothing. I had no idea getting a zoning change would be such a big deal."

Grandpa's face wrinkled with concern. "Are you sure it's worth it?"

Emily nodded. "You and I both know how llama therapy has helped out Klaus."

The first time she had seen her little brother with the llamas, she couldn't believe the change in his demeanor. He didn't speak to the people in his family, but he couldn't stop chattering to Wembley.

"He really is a completely different person around the llamas."

"Exactly. That's why I'm willing to wait out the city for my permit. Eventually someone will understand how important this service will be for the area."

Her grandpa's nose was getting close to the screen again. "I'm proud of you, Emily. I know your parents are, too."

"Thanks, Grandpa." She waved goodbye to the screen and clicked off her phone. She may not have approval from the city yet, but she had all the support she needed from her family. One way or another, she was going to start taking clients before the year was over.

* * *

WHEN WEDNESDAY MORNING CAME, Emily sat up in bed with the nerves of a student before a huge test. It was date day. Her stomach rumbled while she scrambled up eggs for a breakfast burrito, but she couldn't eat more than a couple of bites. She had broken up with her ex seven months before, and been on a handful of bad dates since. Most men weren't capable of pulling their eyes away from their phones long enough to hold a conversation. Porter seemed different.

Emily hopped in her truck and drove a couple of miles down the road to the ranch. She needed a distraction to take her mind off her upcoming date. Checking on the animals wasn't enough to keep her thoughts from wandering back to Porter. She pulled her hair into a ponytail. It was time for a real job.

After rummaging through the shed, Emily found the tool she needed. She threw the saw into the back of her truck and headed to the downed tree. When the chainsaw roared to life, Emily's heart slowed to a steady pulse. It was loud enough to drown out her chaotic thoughts, and just heavy enough that she had to concentrate on the job at hand.

By the time 11:00 rolled around, Emily was covered from head to toe with wood chips and small pieces of leaves. She stood back to survey her progress. Branches were piled high near the fence. It had taken some work, but she had been able to uncover the boards which had been broken when the tree fell, replacing them with new ones.

The knots in her stomach tightened when she looked at her watch. She wondered if she should cancel on Porter. The temptation was strong. There was still a lot of work to do on the ranch, and Emily didn't have time for playing around. After flipping her phone back and forth between her hands, she took a deep breath. People could call Emily any assortment of names, but coward wasn't one of them. She had agreed to a date, and she was going to go no matter how nervous she felt.

She stood in front of her closet, flipping through her shirts. How was she supposed to dress for the date? What if she went too fancy and Porter wore jeans and a button-down shirt? Or if she went casual and he was wearing dress pants? The thought of him dressed up brought a slight flutter to her chest. She needed to stop worrying and call in an expert.

Emily grabbed a couple of different outfits and threw them on the bed, snapping a photo of each one. Then she texted them to her sister.

As expected, her phone rang a minute later.

"Hi Kayla," Emily said. "I need help."

The background noise coming from Kayla's end sounded like a bunch of people cheering in a stadium. "Sorry, Sis. I can't hear you very well."

"Where are you?" Emily asked.

There was a muffled sound and then a door slammed closed. "It's the finals for the ping-pong tournament in the dorm. My guy just scored a point."

"Don't you have classes or something?"

"It's spring break and we were bored."

"I totally forgot about your break. We can talk later," Emily said. She was happy her sister seemed to be thoroughly enjoying her final year of college but her heart fell at the thought of figuring out what to wear on her own.

"It's okay," Kayla said. "I've got a few minutes. What's up with all the outfit pics?"

Emily's pressed her hand to her stomach. If she said the words out loud, there would be no way to back out of the date. Kayla would drive from Colorado to Utah just to make her go.

"It's nothing much. I have a date today and I'm not sure what to wear." She tried to keep her voice level, like it was no big deal.

Kayla's screams were so loud, Emily had to hold the phone away from her ear.

"Tell me everything, Ems. Now."

She took a deep breath. "I met him a couple of days ago. He helped me with a little problem on the ranch."

"Uh huh. That sounds incredibly boring. What aren't you telling me?"

Emily lay down on her bed. "Nothing much, except that he's gorgeous and kind and easy to talk to. I haven't stopped smiling since I met him."

"When did he ask you out?"

"When we were fixing a section of fence. I kind of brushed him off because I'm not looking for anything serious."

"You aren't still hung up on Gabe, are you?"

The name tugged at her heartstrings. "When you date someone for three years that leaves a bit of a mark. But no,

I'm not still hung up on him. It feels like ages since we broke up."

"True. I'm happy you met someone new. I hope the date is awesome." There was a muffled cheer in the background. "Sorry, Sis. They're waving for me to come back. Go with the burgundy shirt and your skinny jeans. The colors will compliment your eyes."

"Thanks, Kayla. You're the best."

"Have fun on your date. I want to hear everything once you are home."

"You'll be the first person I call."

"Love you, Ems."

"Love you too, Sis. I hope your guy wins."

Emily grabbed the outfit Kayla suggested and headed to the bathroom. Hopefully a long, hot shower would ease the tension in her shoulders.

By the time 12:45 rolled around, Emily was dressed. She took a final look in the mirror to make any last-minute adjustments. Her long hair hung down, curling in soft waves. She had debated between the smoky eye look or something simple, choosing a light coat of mascara in the end. No need to stand out if they went somewhere casual. It would look like she was trying too hard for him. The final touch was her favorite lipstick, a light mauve color that brought out the natural blush of her cheeks.

Emily placed her hands on her hips and took a couple of cleansing breaths. If she could handle moving away from family and friends to set up the ranch of her dreams, she could handle a date with a cowboy. Besides, it was nothing more than a simple meal between two friends who had helped each other out after a storm.

Emily glanced down at her phone when she climbed into her truck. It was time to head back to the ranch to wait for the cowboy.

The clock read 1:05 when she pulled into the driveway. Ten minutes was going to have to be long enough to calm the knots in her stomach before Porter showed up. Emily bowed her head and said a quick prayer to steady her nerves. God had helped her out of sticky situations before. He could certainly help her calm down enough to handle a first date.

Emily was tapping her phone on her leg when an email notification appeared from Elk Mountain City Services. Hands shaking, Emily opened her email and clicked on the message.

"Dear Miss Hutchings. We are writing to inform you that your request for the boundary change is under review. Please send the attached items to the city planning department so we can continue to process your request."

Emily's eyes scanned the rest of the message, but the words blurred together. With the city's approval, she'd be able to open her therapy center whenever she was done fixing up the house. They hadn't said yes yet, but it sounded like the city was leaning in that direction. It was going to be a lot of work to get everything ready, but Emily couldn't wait to start meeting with clients again.

She glanced at the clock. Porter was due to arrive any minute. The next five minutes passed in a blur. Emily shot off a quick text to her sister, and then to her grandpa. She pushed the old checkered curtains to the side and looked out the window, but no one was there.

The next ten minutes Emily unpacked a box, stacking books on her bookshelf even though she knew she'd have to move them all when she painted. It made the idea of a front office seem more real. In time, the office would be filled with end tables, chairs, a couch, and a basket of toys for children to play with while they waited for appointments. There were still dozens of things that had to be done before the doors could open.

Emily held off obsessively checking her watch every two minutes until after 1:45 had come and gone. It seemed reasonable to expect some sort of a delay with Porter being a cowboy. Maybe a horse had thrown a shoe or a pig had gotten loose. But when 2:00 rolled around, Emily was fed up. There were acceptable amounts of late, but this was over the line bordering on rude.

When the clock hands moved to the 2:15 position, Emily stormed out of the office. She threw her purse onto the seat of the truck and slammed the door. There were much better ways to spend her time than waiting for a man. Plenty of men had let her down in the past. So much for the cowboy being any different. She didn't need Porter Matthews rubbing it in her face that her time didn't matter.

By the time Emily was nearing home, she was clutching the steering wheel with both hands so tightly, her knuckles were turning white. She wasn't going to waste another minute being angry about being stood up. In the few seconds remaining before the light changed, Emily made a decision. Instead of taking the turn, she stepped on the gas and gunned it through the intersection, going straight until she hit the freeway onramp.

By the time Emily pulled into the hardware store parking lot, her anger was replaced with determination. She didn't have a date to look forward to, but she had an office full of repairs calling her name. Painting the walls was an easy place to start. By the time she had her colors chosen, Porter was pushed to the back of her mind. Hopefully he was enjoying whatever he was doing, because he had blown his chance to get to know her. She didn't have time to give him a second chance.

CHAPTER 5

Porter's night had been restless, with him tossing and turning in bed before falling into a deep sleep close to dawn. When he woke up, he was exhausted but his nerves were calm. He was going to go on a date with Emily, and it was going to be okay. The Lord had spoken peace to his heart in the wee hours of the morning.

The calm feeling followed him through his work. He had gone from task to task, tackling jobs that made his muscles ache. That's why he was extremely confused when he woke up in his room, with the sun slanting through his window from the wrong direction. Where had the day gone and why was he in bed?

He moved to sit up but a wave of nausea forced him to lean back in his pillows and close his eyes, taking deep breaths. He hadn't thrown up for five years and counting, and he wasn't about to start. It wasn't until his head was pressed back against the pillow that he noticed the throbbing along the back of his head. Something was clearly wrong.

"Mom?" he asked. "Anyone?"

Footsteps clipped down the hallway until Reid poked his head through the door. "Hey Port. You're awake."

Porter tried to sit, but the nausea hit with another wave. "What is happening?"

Reid came to sit on the edge of the bed. "Do you remember anything?"

"About what? I remember all sorts of things." Porter turned to his side, holding his stomach.

Reid reached down to the side of the bed and handed Porter a bowl. "You might need this again."

"Again?" So much for the five-year record. "Reid, why am I in bed?"

Reid clamped a hand down on Porter's leg. "You got a concussion, Brother. Rest is the best thing for you right now."

"What do you mean, I got a concussion? I don't remember anything hitting me in the head."

"Mom says that's normal. Your memory should come back."

Porter watched his brother talking, but none of his words were making sense. "Are you going to fill in the blanks? How long have I been out?"

Mom came into the room carrying a tray. She set it down on the nightstand and the smell of chicken vegetable soup filled the room. Porter's stomach lurched. "Thanks, Mom, but there's no way I'm eating that."

"Try a few bites," she said. "It will help calm your

stomach down."

Porter sat up, leaning his head back against the wall. He reached for the spoon, moving slowly in an attempt to keep his stomach calm. When the first sip of soup touched his mouth, his stomach growled with hunger. Maybe his mom was right. He took a couple of bites, and then closed his eyes again.

"I get that I have a concussion, but is anyone going to tell me what happened? Last thing I remember, I was heading to the barn."

Reid shifted on the bed, the movement causing Porter to pull his knees up towards his stomach to keep the soup down.

"Well, we don't really know what happened. You didn't come in to lunch so Mom sent me and Thomas out to find you. We split up, and I found you first. You were laying in the barn, halfway under the tractor, with a bunch of bolts scattered around you. I figured you were trying to fix something."

The memory was fuzzy, but it was starting to come back to Porter. "I was trying to unscrew a bolt from the undercarriage. The wrench slipped and I fell back against something hard. I guess that explains why my head hurts."

Mom reached for his arm. "Your brothers got you home but you need to take it easy for the rest of the day."

"Thanks, guys." Porter ate a couple more bites of soup, letting the broth soothe his stomach. Reid left with their mom and the room fell quiet. Porter reached up to feel the back of his head, wincing when he touched the tender spot. Whatever he hit certainly left a mark.

The sunlight outside was fading quickly. Even though he had been in bed for hours, Porter felt like he could fall asleep and take another nap. He was drifting off to sleep when his eyes snapped open.

Emily. The date. Somehow in his confusion, he had totally forgotten that he made a commitment to her. He reached for his phone, swiping through his contacts to pull up her number. His mind blanked out when he tried to remember her last name so Porter scanned through the names one by one. She wasn't there.

He threw his phone to the bed with a huff. The number had to be there. He'd look again after his head stopped pounding. It wasn't until he closed his eyes again that he realized why he couldn't find her. Between meeting the llamas and fixing the fence, he had forgotten the most basic rule of asking for her number.

Porter lay his head down on the pillow. His agitation was making the room spin. He hoped Emily was a forgiving sort of person. He couldn't imagine that she was happy with him. So much for making a good impression.

* * *

WHEN PORTER SAT up the following morning, he was still exhausted but his mind was clear. He reached back to feel his head, hoping everything had miraculously healed in the night. No such luck. There was a tender spot that hurt when he pressed down lightly. Porter swung his legs to the side of the bed, surprised that none of his brothers were there.

He was walking to the bathroom when Thomas came around the corner.

"What are you doing out of bed?" Thomas asked.

Porter raised an eyebrow at him. "The normal. I think I'm allowed to use the facilities."

Thomas reached for his arm but Porter shook him off. "I promise. I'm doing much better this morning."

His brother studied him, and then shrugged. "You can take it up with Mom. I had the last of the night watch shifts. I'm going back to bed."

"Night watch?"

"Yeah. Mom had us take turns waking you up to make sure you were alive and not too concussed."

That explained part of why Porter felt like he had been run over by a truck. His family hadn't let him sleep.

He jumped into the shower, turning the water as hot as he could handle. The water pounded against his back, loosening up the muscles in his shoulders. Being sore was a normal part of working the ranch, but this was a different kind of tightness. He blamed it on all the tossing and turning he had been doing during the night. Washing his hair was a bit painful, but Porter felt like a new man when he stepped out of the shower and got changed into clean clothes. He headed down the stairs to the kitchen where a chorus of voices babbled.

Mom looked up from where she was cooking. "How are you feeling this morning?"

"Most of the brain fog is gone. I think I'll be fine working today."

She pointed to a chair. "Not a chance, Mister. Your only job is to take it easy."

Porter knew better than to argue with his mom. She had always been protective of her children, but ever since Cassidy's death, she had been extra protective of Porter. He grabbed a plate and held it out, grateful for the food that she served him.

"Do you ever get tired of cooking?" Porter asked.

His mom laughed. "With eight of you guys running around the house? I didn't have much of a choice other than to learn to love it. I'll admit, it is a bit easier cooking when some of the kids are off to college. This week has been busier than normal."

Finn and Wyatt came into the room. "What about this week?"

"I was talking about having to cook extra to feed both of you." Mom waved her spatula towards the twins. Finn dodged around one side while Wyatt grabbed plates from the other.

"You know you miss us when we're at school," Finn said.

She laughed. "Of course, I do. I didn't love it when Porter, Thomas or Reid left for college and I don't love having you gone either. I'm always going to be happy that you are learning though."

Wyatt plopped down at the table next to Porter, scooting his chair so he was right next to his brother's leg. "And what about you, big brother? Did you miss us?"

Porter elbowed Wyatt's ribs. "What? You think I miss all the trouble you guys get into?" He paused, letting the moment stretch out before he grinned at his brother. "I might miss you occasionally. Plus, it's been nice having the extra help this week."

"How's the head?" Finn asked, sitting on the other side of Porter so Porter was penned in. "Do you need us to carry you to the couch when you're done eating?"

Porter looked back and forth between his brothers, rolling his eyes. At times it was exhausting living in a big family, but when pressed, Porter would have to admit that he loved it. He used to think that by this point in his life, he'd be raising several children of his own. He never could have predicted that his wife and first child would pass away, leaving him heartbroken and single with no desire to move on.

Then his dad passed away and Porter's responsibilities at the ranch grew so quickly, he could barely find time to brush his teeth before falling exhausted into bed. Porter knew he wasn't ready for any sort of a relationship after that. He had to accept that he was on a different path than he had originally planned.

Finn reached across Porter and snagged a slice of French toast off of Wyatt's plate. Wyatt smacked his brother's hand.

"Hey, I don't need to be in the middle of this," Porter said. He pushed his chair back and went to sit on the other side of the table. Both brothers looked at him with wide eyes.

"Don't you love us?" Wyatt asked.

"Yeah," Finn said. "Spring break only lasts three more days and then we're going back to school."

Mom set a plate of French toast in the middle of the table. "All right, you two. Stop pestering your brother. There's plenty of food for everyone."

Before long, Thomas and Reid came in and took their seats around the table. Bree joined them a couple of minutes later. Porter scanned the faces of the family he loved. Even though life had taken him on a different path than expected, he couldn't ask for a better support group.

Thomas broke Porter out of his thoughts. "Hey Port? You in there?"

Porter shook his head to clear it. "I was just thinking about how much I appreciate each of you. You make my job a lot easier."

Reid planted his elbows on the table and leaned forward. "Just how hard did you hit your head?"

The front door banged open before Porter could answer. His heart lifted when his remaining siblings walked into the room.

"Hope and Hudson! I thought you guys couldn't make it home this week." Mom was grinning.

"Work decided to let me off early," Hope said. "We weren't going to miss the final days of spring break with all of you."

Hudson set his hat on the edge of the counter and ran a hand through his copper hair. "It was all Hope's idea. I was planning on studying to get caught up, but Hope thought it would be fun to surprise you."

He walked over to Porter's side and reached out to give his big brother a hug. "How are things going over here?"

"You mean apart from the concussion I got yesterday?

We're keeping it together."

"Yeah," Bree said. "Porter was getting all nostalgic on us right before you came in. I think he was just about to tell everyone that I am his favorite sister."

"Oh really?" Hope asked. "I guess I got here just in time to remind him about his real favorite sister."

Hudson raised his eyebrows at Porter. "So, you're picking favorites now?"

Porter shook his head. "Okay, so maybe the concussion got me thinking, but seriously, guys. Do you ever think about where we'd be if Dad were still alive?"

His question brought the laughter and squabbling to a standstill.

"What do you mean?" Mom asked.

"I know none of us wanted Dad to leave. He was gone way too young, but I think it brought us closer together as a family. I can't help but think how different this family would be if Dad were still here." Porter looked around the table, looking each sibling in the eye.

"You're right. I'm guessing at least a few of us would have left the ranch by now," Thomas said. "I'd probably have my own ranch instead of taking care of the horses on this one."

"I'm not sure things would look too different for me," Hope said. "I always wanted to go to college, and now I'm getting ready to graduate. I miss Dad though."

"I miss him, too," Finn said. "But seriously, Porter. How hard did you hit your head? You're not usually this sentimental."

Porter wadded up his napkin and threw it across the

table at Finn's face. "Man, I try to say one nice thing and you guys go crazy."

Hudson and Hope grabbed plates and joined the family at the table. Porter leaned back in his chair, watching his siblings as they laughed, reached across the table for food, and talked animatedly with their hands. He looked at his mom, taking in the joy she had on her face while she was surrounded by her children.

Before long, the French toast was gone. The laughter from breakfast turned towards conversations about the chores of the day. Mom Matthews stood up from the table and began to clear away the plates. She walked to the kitchen and Finn, Hudson, and Bree followed behind.

Porter smiled when the clanging of dishes in the sink echoed down the hall. He stayed at the table, waiting until the hubbub calmed down. When everyone scattered to do their work, Mom came back into the room.

"What's on your mind?" she asked.

"I need your help with something." Porter said.

* * *

THE SUN WAS high overhead when Porter and his mom headed to the car. The last time he asked his mom to drive him to meet a girl, he was fourteen. He thought that by thirty-three the nerves would have eased up, but the thought of talking to Emily had his palms sweating. It would be easy to blame the heat on the car, but the spring weather had yet to warm up.

Mom reached out a hand and pressed down lightly on

Porter's knee which was jiggling up and down. "You're really nervous about this, aren't you?"

He opened his mouth to contradict her before his mind could catch up to his heart. "A little bit. I stood her up yesterday, and that's not something I do."

"I'm sure she'll understand when you explain why."

Porter wanted to agree, except for the knot in his stomach that wouldn't go away no matter which way he looked at the situation. "Mom, did you ever think about dating again after Dad died?"

She turned her head to glance Porter's way and then looked back out the front window. "I don't know. I have children and a house and thirty-five years of memories wrapped up in a marriage. I'm not sure I want to start over building something new with someone else."

"It sounds like you've thought about it at least a little bit." Porter said.

"I have. If the right person came along, I would hope my heart would be open enough to give him half a chance."

The words were soothing to Porter. "I keep telling myself that this date with Emily wasn't a big deal, but then I feel awful that I didn't follow through. I don't want to be someone who disappoints her."

Mom nodded her head. "I think that says a lot about your character." She pulled the car off the road and followed the gravel driveway until she came to a stop next to Emily's truck.

Porter's heart sped up. "Here goes nothing." He got out of the car and walked to the front door, straightening out his hat before he raised his hand to knock.

CHAPTER 6

Emily was midway through the chorus of her favorite song, belting out the words with gusto, when she heard the faint knock of someone at the door. She looked down at the paint roller in her hand and pushed the hair out of her eyes, fairly certain she was leaving a streak of paint behind. The air conditioning guy was early for once. She had expected him to arrive on normal maintenance-worker timing.

The interruption to her song would be worth it if he could give her an estimate that fit her budget, even if he was interrupting her right when the song was reaching the best part. Emily turned down the music with a small frown. She'd have to start the play list again once the AC guy was gone. The painting went so much faster when she could sing loudly to her music.

The knocking was much louder now that her music was turned down to a normal decibel. "Hold on a sec," she called. She paused at the edge of the room to slip out of her paint-splattered shoes. There was no sense tracking paint across the hardwood flooring until she decided if she was going to restore it.

Emily looked down to make sure the paint on her hands was dry before she reached for the knob. Standing on the porch was the last person in the universe that she expected to see.

"Porter," she said. In the briefest of seconds her mind registered that she was standing in front of an incredibly handsome man wearing her rattiest t-shirt, paint-splattered pants from high school, and no makeup. Her hair was pulled back into a bun but it didn't take a mirror to guess that there were small clumps of paint dotting her hair. She hadn't exactly been careful when painting the ceiling.

She cleared her throat and tried again. "You are not the AC guy." It took a lot of will power to hold his gaze when his hazel eyes watched her with a twinkle. He looked distractingly good, in a way that was making her forget that she was actually angry with him. She was so focused on his face; she didn't see the person in the car to the side of Porter until the woman shifted in her seat and waved out the window.

Porter's smile lit his eyes. "I'm not the AC guy, but if you're having a problem, I'd be happy to take a look."

Emily took a step back. "Um, what are you doing here? And who is the woman with you?"

He glanced towards the car. "Oh. That's my mom. She drove me here."

Emily pressed her thumb and forefinger against the sides of her nose, trying to make sense of the situation. "Why did you need a ride? Is your truck still broken?" Even with a broken truck, Porter should have been able to borrow his mom's car. Why did he need a chauffeur?

Porter leaned forward and put his hand on the side of the door frame. "It's a bit of a story. Can we talk?"

With the cowboy standing in front of her, Emily remembered why she was painting the house in the first place. "We were supposed to go on a date yesterday."

"We were."

"And you stood me up." Emily was working to keep her tone level. She wasn't going to yell with Porter's mom sitting nearby in a car.

"I did. I can explain." Porter shifted so his shoulder was resting against the door frame. "Can I come in?"

Emily wanted to turn him down. Letting Porter in would be going against her no second chances policy, but what was she supposed to do with his mom right there? She didn't even know the woman but she didn't want to look like a bad person.

"I'm kind of in the middle of something."

Porter nodded. "I'll be quick." He watched her with his mesmerizing eyes, and Emily found herself nodding.

"You've got five minutes. Does your mom want to come in too?"

He shook his head. "Nah. She's used to waiting in the car for kids."

The words made Emily's stomach tighten. "Are you one

of those guys who lives in the basement eating Ramen every day while your mom does your laundry?"

Porter's eyes got big. "How did you know?" He stuffed his hands in his pockets and looked at the ground.

Emily's heart sank. "Oh. Crap." There wasn't anything to say. He seemed so much more put together than that. Now she wasn't sure she wanted him coming in.

The air seemed thicker when Porter looked back at Emily. Then a small smile lifted the corner of his mouth. "I do live with my mom, but that is because my dad passed away a few years ago and she needed the help. If you've been to the ranch, you'd know there is no Ramen to be seen anywhere. My mom is an amazing cook."

His explanation punched Emily in the gut. "I'm sorry for your loss."

Porter rubbed his brow. "Thank you. But that's not why I'm here."

He was right. It was time to get the conversation over with. Emily opened the door, but she wasn't sure where to put Porter. The office had chairs, but sitting would invite a longer conversation which she didn't have time for. He was the one who stood her up after all. She walked partway into the entryway and spun around so she could face him.

"This is far enough. What do you have to tell me?"

Porter reached up and took his hat off. He ran his fingers through his hair, stopping with a small wince when he reached the back of his head. "I was actually excited to take you out. Well, honestly kind of terrified but excited too."

He had been excited? So had she, until he'd bailed. "If you were excited, what happened?"

Porter's mouth pulled into a small frown. "I was working on the tractor and managed to fall back and hit my head. Apparently, I hurt myself pretty badly because the next thing I knew, I was stuck in my bed and the day was over."

Emily studied his face. "You don't look like you've got any injuries."

"Yeah. Except for a moderate concussion."

The pieces were clicking into place. "Is that why your mom is driving you around?"

"Yep. She won't let me drive until she thinks I'm better. She's been a bit overprotective since. . ." He trailed off. "Well, for a long time."

Emily needed a minute to sort her feelings. She didn't give second chances but Porter hadn't really lost the first chance on his own. He had a pretty good excuse. "How are you feeling now?" She felt like a jerk for not asking him to sit while they talked.

"The back of my head is tender and some of the details surrounding the accident are a little fuzzy, but mostly I feel fine." He held his hat, turning it over in his hands.

"You didn't need to come all the way over here." Emily wanted to pat his arm and tell him it would be okay, but she wasn't that forward.

"Commitments mean something to me. I wanted you to know why I bailed."

"You could have texted." A flicker of anger flared up.

Even if he was injured, he should have been able to send a quick message.

Porter's eyes had a twinkle that was making it hard for her to keep her frustration brewing. "I tried to text you last night. It didn't work so well when I realized I didn't have your number."

Emily's mouth puckered into a circle. "How did we miss that?"

"I'm going to blame the llamas. They threw me off my game." Porter stepped back so he was leaning against the hallway wall.

"You're suggesting that the guy who had his mommy drive him here has game?"

Porter's answering grin made her heart flutter.

"Hey. At least I'm trying to make things right. Even if my mom had to help."

Emily looked towards the door. "I don't want to keep her waiting. Are you sure she doesn't want to come in?"

"Nah. I told her I'd be just a few minutes."

The thought of Porter leaving so soon made Emily's heart twinge. She had been ready to write him off moments before, but somehow, he had the ability to calm her racing nerves. She was standing in front of him looking like she'd stepped out of a painting commercial gone wrong, but it didn't bother her.

Porter scuffed his boot along the floor. "So, would it be okay if I got your number now?" He glanced down at the floor and then lifted his eyes to meet hers. Was he actually nervous?

Emily pulled out her phone. "Let's do it." She typed

Porter's name into her phone, knowing that the first time he showed up on her screen, she was going to smile. She held up her phone to snap a picture for the contacts.

"Hey, no fair taking my picture when I'm concussed."

Emily lowered her hand and rolled her eyes. "I imagine you look exactly the same as you always do."

"Ruggedly handsome?" Porter asked, winking.

He was spot on, but she wasn't going to admit that. "You look like the same cowboy who helped me fix my fence a few days ago." She didn't add that he made her insides squirm like a love-sick woman who hadn't had a real relationship in a long time. Or that whenever he fixed his eyes on her, she had to remind herself how to form coherent sentences.

Emily turned away from Porter to look down the hall. She had left the paint bucket open and her roller out. As much as she would enjoy chatting in the hallway, she had a job to do. When she turned back, Porter's phone was up and he was snapping her picture.

"No way," she said. She lunged for the phone in Porter's hand but he held it high above her head, an impish grin on his face. "You can't take a picture of me when I look like this."

"I don't know," Porter said. "I think the paint adds a certain charm. He lowered the phone and tucked it into his pocket. "Now, are you going to show me what you are working on?"

Emily was smart enough to know when it was time to stop fighting. She turned down the hallway and headed to the first room. Some of the walls still sported the deep mustard yellow that the previous owners had chosen, but the wall closest to the door was now a crisp eggshell white.

Porter studied the walls. "You sure you don't want to keep the original color? You've got a piece of history here. I'm not sure they even make that color of paint anymore."

"It was tempting, but I decided to go with something more neutral since this is going to be an office. I want my therapists to have more choices for decorating."

"I see." Porter stepped to the middle of the room and turned in a slow circle. "You want some help?"

Emily did, but she wasn't going to admit it. "I'm pretty sure your mom isn't going to want to wait outside while we work."

"No, but I bet she wouldn't mind coming back later." Porter raised an eyebrow. "What do you think?"

The question raced through Emily's mind. She wasn't sure she was ready to commit to an afternoon with Porter. Especially when he couldn't leave unless someone picked him up. She opened her mouth to say no, but the word yes popped out instead.

"Alright. I'll be right back." Porter walked out of the room and Emily leaned against the wall to catch her breath. If she wasn't careful, her attraction to Porter was going to turn into a full-blown crush.

When Porter walked back into the room, Emily had to turn away to hide the heat rising on her face. Somewhere between the trip to the car and coming back, he had taken off his long-sleeved shirt so he was wearing just a t-shirt that stretched across his chest. It was obvious that Porter had built up a good set of muscles working on the ranch.

Emily headed to the corner and grabbed a handle from her supplies. She attached a roller and handed it over to Porter. "You can start on that wall." She pointed to a spot on the opposite side of the room. Then she dipped her own roller in the paint and got back to work. Handsome distraction or not, Emily had a job to do.

CHAPTER 7

Porter obediently stepped to the wall that Emily pointed to, but after a few minutes, the awkward silence filling the room became too heavy for him. He dipped his roller in the tray, filling it with a good amount of paint. Then he walked over to Emily's side of the room. "Race you?"

He had gotten a good idea of Emily's character a couple of days ago. If he had judged her right, she didn't seem like the kind of woman who'd back down from a challenge. Sure enough, she took a step back from the wall to stare at him.

"Doing what?" she asked.

"We start on opposite sides of the wall. First person to the center wins."

Emily tapped the handle of the roller in her hand. "You're on. How do you feel about music?"

Porter tried to suppress his grin. "Like the song I heard you belting out earlier?"

"Ugh. I hoped you didn't hear that." A pretty flush tipped her ears.

"Hey, you're not the only one with a set of lungs. You pick the music; I'll get our trays ready."

While Emily busied herself with the speaker at the far end of the room, Porter carefully poured paint to top off each tray. He made sure the levels were exactly the same so they were starting on even footing. He wasn't going to stand accused of cheating. When Emily came back, he grabbed a quarter out of his pocket.

"Heads or tails?" He held the coin up.

Emily started laughing. "For what?"

"Hey, when I win this contest, I want it to be fair and square. We're flipping this coin to choose which side of the wall to start on."

"You're crazy." Emily tapped her chin. "Who's calling it?"

Porter grinned. "Your call." He flipped the quarter, catching it midair.

"Tails," Emily said.

Porter smacked the coin down on his arm, lifting his hand to reveal the verdict.

"Tails!" Emily did a little jump. "I win. I choose the left side."

"I'm pretty sure that just sealed your fate. The right side clearly has the advantage." Porter walked to his tray, flexing with his roller. He was flirting with Emily, and it felt good.

"I hope you're not a sore loser." Emily pressed a button on her phone and loud music filled the room.

"We Are the Champions?" Porter held back a snort.

Emily got extra points for the snark. He waited for her cue.

Emily settled into a slight lunge. "Alright. Ready, set, go."

Porter began to paint the wall in front of him, trying to keep pace with Emily. He had the longer arm span, but she had clearly been doing a lot more painting than him. When Emily went to her paint tray to refill the roller, it took her less than half the time he took. It was going to be a close call.

He was cruising right along until Emily started to sing. Her voice shot right to his heart, making him want to grab her in his arms and pull her close for a dance. Instead, he took a gulp and sang along, belting out the words to the song.

The look on Emily's face made it worth it. She paused her painting to watch Porter, and he took advantage of the moment. He painted his side of the wall, getting closer and closer to the center line. He could say his motivation was to win the contest, but an unexpected side effect was every step bringing him closer to Emily.

They made it to the center of the room at the same time. Porter painted the wall above Emily's head while she painted the wall below, both rollers flying across the wall. Then they straightened up.

Porter's shoulder muscles were sore and his head was beginning to throb slightly when he stepped to the center of the room to survey his work. He looked at Emily for approval, raising his eyebrow. "So? Who wins?"

He could see her trying to suppress a smile that danced

along her lips. Then a frown crept in. Emily pointed to part of the wall.

Porter followed her finger, noticing a square patch on his side that had a faint yellow tint. In his frantic race to the middle, he had missed one spot.

"I'm pretty sure this means you've been eliminated." Emily placed her hand on his arm. "It was a valiant effort, but you just don't have what it takes to beat me."

"You're right. I fold. I do take care of my mistakes though." He stepped towards the paint tray but Emily cut him off. Porter tried to stop his forward momentum but he was too late. His hand swung down against the edge of the tray while Emily was lifting it, and the results were disastrous. Porter watched the tray flying towards his chest, but he didn't have time to react before paint was dripping down the front of his clothes.

Emily's face froze in shock. She stretched her hand towards him and then pulled it back. "I'm so sorry," she said.

Porter reached for a rag and began to dab at the mess. The cold paint seeped through his shirt to his skin. He was pretty sure his stomach was a nice eggshell white. That was going to be interesting to wash off later. The shirt was definitely ruined, but the day didn't have to be.

Emily still wasn't moving. Porter rested his hand lightly on the top of her shoulder. "It was an accident. Just as much my fault as yours."

"But. Your clothes." She gestured to his shirt, not finishing her sentence.

The mood in the room had dropped from light hearted

singing to a heaviness that Porter didn't like. He needed to make things right. "Hey, look at me."

Emily lifted her eyes to his.

"This right here?" He gestured to the front of his shirt. "This is any given Tuesday for me. If I'm not dousing myself with paint, I'm tromping through the mud or smearing grease on my clothes. Life as a rancher isn't exactly a clean job." He wanted to get back to the familiar feeling of laughing together.

A moment later, her shoulders relaxed and she let out a deep breath. "You're right. I still feel bad. I'd offer you a shirt to change into, but I don't think we're quite the same size."

Porter picked up another rag and swiped it across his shirt. "It'll be dry in no time." Then he reached for his roller.

"Hey, I've got it," Emily said. This time she held his arm back while she stepped forward. She dipped her roller in the paint, and with a quick flick of her wrist, she applied the final coat. This time, when they stepped back to inspect, the yellow tint was gone.

Porter could see Emily sneaking glances at her watch. "Am I keeping you from something?" he asked.

She rubbed her forehead. "I'm trying to decide if I have time to start painting the next room before I need to feed the animals. I don't like to make them wait too long."

Porter could feel his time with Emily slipping away. "Want any help feeding them?" He plunged his roller in a bucket of water.

Emily planted her hands on her hips. "I know I didn't

really talk to your mom today, but I'm pretty sure taking her concussed son out to do hard labor would earn me a scolding. I probably shouldn't have even let you paint."

A surge of happiness shot through Porter. If Emily was worried about what his mom thought, she was starting to feel comfortable with him again. "So, you want me to call for my chauffeur?"

The room was still for a moment. Then Emily lowered her hands from her hips. "I'd hate for your mom to have to make an extra trip. If you're cool waiting around in those painted clothes a bit longer, I can take you home after I feed the animals."

Porter glanced down at his t-shirt. The paint was already starting to dry, but even if it hadn't been, he was in. "Deal."

* * *

THE SUN WAS DIPPING towards the mountains, casting a harsh light on the side of the barn Porter leaned against. He didn't want to admit it, but he was starting to feel tired and it was barely late afternoon. Even though his head was starting to throb, not helping Emily to do her chores was taking all his will power. His dad taught him that a proper cowboy always helped when there was work to be done. Sitting on his hands was a feeling Porter wasn't used to.

He watched Emily fill the water buckets from a spigot near the barn. "You said you got your first llama from your grandma's friend, right?"

"My grandpa's friend. I lost my grandma when I was five."

"Oh. I'm sorry. I didn't know." Porter hated talking about death with people. It usually made them treat him differently. Society accepted losing relatives when they were in their older years. Porter had lost two people who were entirely too young to go, and that made people worry about saying the wrong thing. He took a quick breath, waiting for Emily's comment that would change the vein of their lighthearted conversation, but it didn't come. She was new enough to town, she must not have heard about Cassidy.

Emily looked up from the water spigot. "It's okay. I'll tell you about her one day because she was pretty awesome. Anyway, what was your question? Something about the llamas?"

Porter let out his breath. "I was going to ask where you learned to take care of them. I've been on a ranch for years and I don't think I'd know what to do."

The water bucket was filled almost to the top. Emily turned off the spigot and stepped to the side of the pen. "I learned a lot from helping my grandpa's friend, but I also spent a ton of time searching the internet to find tips. Did you know that if you search llama care, there is a page dedicated entirely to what kind of headwear llamas prefer? There is some interesting stuff out there."

Emily walked towards the pasture, lugging the water bucket, and Porter followed behind. Being unable to help with the heavy lifting didn't mean that he had to stay quiet.

"From what I've seen today, they mostly just free-forage, right?"

"Yep. I'm glad the spring grasses are finally starting to grow back so they can graze again. I can supplement with hay when I need to but I like them getting their exercise out in the fields."

"And you take care of these guys all by yourself?"

Emily turned away from Porter to look at the mountains. Then she turned back. "I didn't in the past." She poured the bucket into a trough and walked back to the spigot near the barn. "It's been an adjustment living here without my family around."

Porter could sense that Emily was holding back her story, but he didn't want to push her too hard. He certainly had his share of things he wasn't ready to share with her, no matter how charming she was. "So, instead of using family, you've got a concussed cowboy following you around, pestering you with questions." He raised an eyebrow. "Am I close?"

Emily rolled her eyes. "I'm not sure what I did to deserve this punishment. Last I checked, I was behaving pretty well."

"Well, apparently not because you're stuck with me." Being stuck with Emily was a punishment Porter was happy to take.

"Your turn," Emily said.

"For what?"

"You've been asking me questions ever since we fed the horses on the other side of the ranch. My turn to learn about you."

Porter's stomach clenched. He wasn't ready to answer anything serious but he couldn't lie to Emily. "What do you want to know?"

Emily rubbed her hands together. "You live with your mom, right?"

"Yep. And a few other siblings."

That earned an eyebrow raise. "Huh. I met Thomas briefly. Who are the other ones?"

Porter took a deep breath and rattled off the siblings in age order. "Me, Thomas, Reid, Hudson, Hope, Finn, Wyatt and Bree."

Emily's mouth dropped open. "Wow. They all live at the house right now?"

"Not usually. Hudson, Hope, Finn and Wyatt are off to college but they came home for spring break." He looped his thumbs through his belt loops. "How about you? Do you have any siblings?"

Emily shook her head. "Yes. Two, but it's not my turn. You're answering the questions. Remember?"

"Right. What else do you want to know?"

He watched Emily's face, taking in the specks of paint that dotted her cheeks like freckles. Between his paint-covered shirt and her speckled hair, they were quite a sight to see. The heavy lifting brought a red tint to Emily's cheeks that made her endearing to watch. When she turned her eyes to meet his, there was a softness behind the look.

Porter braced himself for the question he figured was coming next.

"Do you mind telling me about your dad? From the

little bits you've told me about your mom, she sounds like a pretty incredible woman. What was your dad like?"

A lump filled Porter's throat. "He was one of a kind. I swear, he could do anything he set his mind to."

"Like what?" Emily walked over to the barn and stacked her buckets by the wall.

"Let's see. One year there was a serious drought. Ranches all around us were having to shut down and skimp on operations. My dad was determined to see us through the rough patch."

"What did he do?"

"He spent hours every day checking the crops. He worked out a crazy rotation schedule working through the nights to avoid the worst evaporation times of day. We barely survived that summer, but a number of the ranches around us really suffered. A few even went under."

If Porter closed his eyes, he could still hear his dad's voice calling for him to wake up in the middle of the night. Working in the fields round the clock made Porter crazy, but now he was grateful for his dad's dedication. They had a sprawling ranch that was thriving thanks to the work ethic his dad had pounded into all the kids.

Emily took a step closer to Porter and his heart kicked up a notch. He wasn't used to standing so close to a woman who made his pulse race. She didn't look at him like he was damaged goods.

"What happened to him?" Emily placed her hand on his arm. "Or is that too personal a question?" She lowered her hand and stepped back.

Porter slipped his hands into his pockets so he wouldn't

reach out and pull Emily close to his chest. "I don't mind talking about it. He and my brother Hudson loved working the rodeo circuit. It was a simple accident, really. One minute he was doing a practice run, and the next he was flying off his horse."

The words were bringing back all of Porter's emotion from that day. He blinked up at the sky, determined not to tear up in front of Emily. After a quick count to three, Porter cleared his throat and looked back down. "The doctors say it was a one in a million chance that he would land the way he did, but my dad was always defying the odds. This time, they weren't on his side. He didn't make it to the hospital."

Emily's face fell. She came forward and wrapped her arms around Porter's waist. "Oh, Porter. I'm so sorry. I shouldn't have asked."

Porter rested his hand on her back, enjoying the tingle that ran through his body while holding her close. If this was what being open with Emily felt like, maybe he was ready to open his heart again.

He waited until she broke the hug and stepped back. "Okay. Enough of the sad stuff. What else do you want to know?" Eventually he'd have to tell her about Cassidy, but this wasn't the day.

CHAPTER 8

Emily couldn't believe Porter had been so open with her. She had asked some pretty personal questions that she half expected him to shy away from. He was continuing to break her expectations. It wasn't until Emily got home and looked in the mirror that she decided Porter may have just been pitying her.

No one could accuse Emily of being a vain woman. She loved getting the job done. If that meant ending the day with mud on her boots and a streak of dirt on her cheek, so be it. It was part of the job. Yet seeing the person in the mirror made her shake her head. With the amount of paint splattered on her body, it was a wonder any of it got on the walls. Their contest should have been who could wear the most paint.

The following day the thought of Porter sent a flutter through Emily's chest. She had gotten pretty good at keeping her head down and working, not padding in any time for dating. Her last boyfriend had stuck around just long enough for the first emergency on the ranch to crop up. Then he high-tailed it out of there, leaving her to take care of three very sick llamas. The llamas healed, but the relationship did not.

One thing she had proven over the years was that she was strong enough to do everything on her own. She didn't need a man to take care of her. So why did Porter's rugged face keep drifting into her thoughts while she opened the paint cans? Why did the thought of his arms make her wish they were wrapped around her waist instead of holding a paint roller? Emily shook her head to clear her mind, but it didn't do much good. As soon as her mind settled down, he drifted back into her thoughts.

If her mind was going to keep misbehaving, there was only one thing to do. Emily pulled out her phone and pressed on the Porter icon. Her stomach turned into a tangled swarm of butterflies as the phone rang, but there was no turning back. When Porter answered the phone, Emily gulped.

"Hi Porter. It's Emily."

His low chuckle sent a wave of courage through her.

"I guessed as much, unless one of the llamas took your phone. My bets are on Bonnie figuring it out."

"Right. I forgot about caller ID." Emily cleared her throat. Her mind went blank about her excuse for calling. She and Porter hadn't exactly established a chatting relationship yet. A quick glance around the office gave her the inspiration she needed.

"So, this is a strange question, but do you happen to have a membership to the big Cost Club warehouse?"

"I do. Why?"

Emily swallowed, reminding herself that she was a grown adult who had plenty of experience talking to handsome men. "They are having a sale on a couch that I'd like to get for the office but I don't want to buy a membership when I'm shopping for one. I can't seem to eat my way through most of the bulk items."

"I see." Porter's voice sounded amused.

"I was hoping you could help me buy the couch and bring it here. I'll buy you lunch as a thank you."

"Hold on." There was a muffled sound on the other end of the phone and Emily could hear a murmur of voices. Then Porter was back. "I can pick you up in an hour. Does that work for you?"

Emily pumped her fist in the air. "I'll be ready. Thank you." She hung up the phone and did a happy dance. It was going to be good to see the cowboy again.

The hour flew by. Before Emily knew it, Porter was pulling into the driveway. He climbed down from the truck and Emily's mouth went dry. He was wearing a clean, pale green t-shirt and faded blue jeans, with a brown pair of boots. She walked down the steps to greet him, trying to ignore the way his hair danced in the wind.

"Was there any chance of salvaging your shirt from yesterday?" she asked.

"Nope. It's a goner." Porter ran a hand through his hair, a smile on his lips.

"Well, thanks for agreeing to help me." Emily walked beside him to the truck. "I promise to not throw paint on you today."

"No problem." Porter laughed. "Besides, I asked Finn to watch things so I've got a couple of hours to spare. It's good for him to have something to do."

Emily nodded. "Awesome. Let's do this." She climbed into the truck, turning her head to the side so she could discretely breathe in the woodsy scent that was uniquely Porter.

He pulled on his seatbelt and put the truck in reverse. "One Cost Club coming up."

Emily's palms began to sweat as they pulled away from the ranch. She had worked so hard to finish things on her own, and the first chance she got, she was asking the cowboy for help. "I didn't want to call you," she said.

Porter glanced her way. "Oh really? Why?"

Emily rubbed her hands on her pants. "It's kind of a pride thing. I want to be able to say that I built this center on my own."

The side of Porter's mouth lifted. "Does using my membership card even count? I mean, I can let you heft the couch up the stairs yourself if that helps."

He was joking, but it was almost tempting. Emily turned in her seat so she could see Porter's face better. "I don't know. I guess maybe I'll let you help with some of the lifting. I'll pretend that you're one of the Cost Club employees."

"Deal." Porter turned the truck onto the highway, heading towards the center of town. He began to hum as he drove.

Emily reached for the radio knob. "Mind if I turn it on?" she asked. She didn't want to suffer through an awkward drive to the store if they ran out of things to talk about.

He raised an eyebrow and then gestured to the panel. "It's all yours."

Emily pushed the buttons, curious to see what Porter's favorite channels were. The first two stations were country music. No surprise there. The next one was playing a top forty countdown. That seemed reasonable for the cowboy as well. It was the fourth button she pushed that gave her pause.

"Gospel hip hop?" she guessed after listening for a minute.

Porter's sheepish grin made her stomach flutter. "What can I say? I love the sound of hip hop but I'm not a big fan of the lyrics. This is a good compromise." Porter lifted his hand to his mouth like a microphone and began to sing along. By the time they were pulling into the Cost Club parking lot, Emily had tears of laughter rolling down her face.

After he put the car in park, Porter turned to face her. "Are you ready?"

Emily wiped the tears from the corners of her eyes. "Let's do this." She walked beside Porter, trying to ignore the raised eyes and whispers of the people who walked past. Finally, Emily had enough. She pulled Porter's arm to a stop.

"Do I have something on my face?" she asked. "Or do I still have paint in my hair?"

Porter looked at her carefully, his scrutiny sending a

tidal wave of nerves rushing through her body. "I don't think so," he finally said. "Why?"

Emily waited until another group finished walking past. "People keep giving me strange looks."

Understanding crossed Porter's face. "About that. You know this is a small town, right?"

"Yeah."

"Well, pretty much anytime anyone shows up with a new person, the town gets talking. I can guarantee that we're going to be the subject of a few dinner table conversations tonight."

Heat flooded Emily's cheeks. "I'm so sorry. I didn't know." She looked at the ground, embarrassed that she put him in such an awkward situation.

Porter nudged her side with his elbow. His adorable grin helped to calm Emily's nerves. "I knew what I was getting into. Let them talk. Our only business here is to worry about buying that couch for your office."

Although he made a good point about not worrying, Emily breathed a sigh of relief when they turned down the furniture aisle. There were less people around, which meant less staring.

Emily was debating between two couches when Porter tapped her on the shoulder. "I'll be back in just a minute, okay?"

"No problem. I'll be here." Emily felt the fabrics of both couches. She wasn't sure which kind would hold up best in the waiting room of the therapy center. It was reasonable to expect at least a few kids would jump on the furniture, no matter how much their parents tried to encourage them to be still.

Moments later a mound of pillows appeared around the corner, with long legs attached. Emily watched, amused, as Porter tried to walk without bumping into anything.

"Need a hand?" Emily asked.

Porter peered around the side of the pillows and grinned. "Almost there," he said. He walked a few more steps and dumped the pillows onto the couches.

"And what, pray tell, are you doing?" Emily put her hands on her hips and tried to scowl, but she could feel the smile dancing on her lips.

"You can't buy a couch unless you try out all the features." Porter spread the pillows to the corners of the first couch and held his hand out. "After you."

The scowl wasn't going to last. Emily burst out laughing and sat down, trying to act casual when Porter plopped down beside her. "And those features are?"

"Firmness of the cushions?" Porter was looking at Emily with his eyebrows raised.

"Uh, this one is a little hard but it's not bad." Emily slouched down on the couch, scooting her body to the edge of the cushion so she could lay her head on the backrest. "Scratch that. This one does not give off very comforting vibes."

"Vibes?" Porter asked. He held out a pillow which she tucked behind her neck. "Does this help?"

They were sitting in the middle of a giant warehouse, but all Emily could concentrate on was the man sitting beside her. She guessed that the couch would always feel comfortable if there was a Porter that came with it. She shook her head. "I'm not sure."

"Okay. So not too comforting on the vibes." Porter began to bounce up and down.

"Now what are you doing?"

"I'm testing the springs. I don't hear any creaking." Porter stopped bouncing and slid his hand down the arm rest. "The fabric is smooth."

"It's okay, but I'm not sure I'm a fan. Let's try the other one." Emily watched a young child run by, being chased by a somewhat harried looking mother. That was one person who probably wouldn't go home to gossip about her and Porter. A teenager followed behind with a cart, a bored expression on her face.

Once the family had turned to the next aisle, Emily grabbed her pillow and walked to the other couch. She turned to Porter. "Ready? On the count of three. One. Two. Three. Sit!"

They flopped down on the couch together, ending up with less than an inch of space between them. Heat shot through Emily's body but then Porter shifted to the side, putting a little space between them. Although she liked this couch much better, it was difficult to say if that was because the cushions were more comfortable or if it was because of the handsome man sitting next to her.

Emily closed her eyes, trying to imagine how the couch would look in the foyer.

"We have to test one more thing," Porter said.

"Okay." Emily was trying to picture an end table that

would fit in the room when Porter stood up. He pulled a patio chair to the other side of the aisle and asked Emily to sit there. She laughingly obliged. Then Porter lay on the couch, propping his head and his feet up on pillows. If the neighbors weren't talking yet, they would be when they saw this.

Porter watched her with a mischievous glint in his eyes.

"I'm confused," Emily said. "What, exactly, are we testing here? Nap time?"

The smile that crossed Porter's face was infectious.

"You're a therapist, right? I'm ready for my session."

Emily jumped off the patio chair and shoved Porter's boots off the couch with a laugh. "I did mention this is for the waiting room, right? Besides, that whole laying on the couch and talking to the therapist bit doesn't work so well when you're including a llama in the session."

"Good point," Porter said. "I guess I'm out of tests, then."

Emily tossed a pillow towards his face. "I'm pretty sure I'm not counting this as actual help. Even with your membership card."

Porter sat up straight. "That's fair. So, are you ready to decide?"

Emily didn't want to leave yet. "We haven't tested how it feels if someone has to wait for more than a minute. Sometimes therapy sessions run long."

"True." Porter raised his eyebrows. "What do you suggest?"

Emily shifted in the seat until she was more comfortable. "You could tell me a story. Tell me something about you that I don't know."

Porter folded his hands in his lap. "Like what."

"Anything. What's the bravest thing you've ever done?" Emily figured he'd have at least a few stories from working on the ranch.

"The truth?" Porter asked.

"Definitely."

Porter rubbed his chin. "It's not a pretty story."

Now she was intrigued. "You don't have to tell me if you don't want to."

Porter closed his eyes and let out a deep breath. "It happened about twelve years ago."

Emily folded her hands in her lap. Then she unfolded them and placed one on her knee. She was ready to listen.

CHAPTER 9

Porter couldn't believe he was sitting on a couch with Emily in the middle of Cost Club. She wanted to know his bravest moment but he couldn't tell her about burying Cassidy and Claire. Getting out of bed that next day was the bravest thing he had ever done, but he wasn't ready to share that story with Emily yet.

Luckily, there was a different story that would work. Porter rubbed his hands on his pants, trying to calm the nerves that were shooting through his body.

"Growing up on a ranch is a lot different than growing up in a city. As kids, we ran around with very little supervision. My parents figured we'd all watch out for each other, and for the most part we did. I think as we grew older, my mom appreciated having other adults around to help out with the younger ones."

"That sounds kind of ideal," Emily said. When she watched him with her pretty eyes, he didn't feel any judgment.

"For the most part, it was." Porter closed his eyes, letting the memory of those days wash over him.

"One Christmas I came home from college and all I wanted to do was blow off some steam. Finals had been a nightmare, and I was ready for a break. Thomas, Reid, and I decided to go check the pond to see if it was frozen over enough for us to pull out our ice skates."

Emily began to laugh.

"What did I say?"

She covered her mouth with her hand. "Sorry. I'm trying to picture you on ice skates. The image of you out there with your cowboy hat on is amusing."

Porter scooted all the way to the edge of the couch. He crossed his arms over his chest before he turned to face Emily. "I bet I could skate circles around you."

Emily raised her hands in surrender. "I'm sure you can. Sorry. I'm ready to listen again."

Porter raised his eyebrows. "You promise?"

She crossed her fingers and held them up. "Cross my heart."

Pulling out the memory was making Porter's stomach tight. "I had been looking forward to playing on the ice with my brothers. We were halfway to the pond when we heard a small voice yelling at us to wait."

The next part of the story filled Porter with shame. "I'd like to say we were good brothers and we waited for Bree, but we didn't."

Emily sat up straight, her eyes wide. "How old was she?"

"She was four. I feel awful about it now, but back then I

was selfish and didn't care. She stopped yelling for us to wait so we figured she had given up and gone back home."

Emily shook her head back and forth. "So, you made it to the pond without your little sister. Was the ice ready for skating?"

"Nope. The pond wasn't quite frozen yet. Instead, we spent our time throwing snowballs at each other and having stupid races. It was a blast."

Emily grabbed a pillow and pulled it to her chest. "Why do I feel like there is a bad ending to this story?"

"Well, you did ask for a story about bravery."

"True."

Porter rubbed his hands on his jeans. "The brave part comes soon. As I was saying, we were having a blast. We played until we knew our dad would be wanting help with the chores. That was when we decided to head home."

Porter closed his eyes and shuddered; the next part of the story seared into his memory. "We were laughing and wrestling back and forth until we got to the final curve of the path. Bree was sitting there, her hands wrapped around her knees."

The sharp intake of Emily's breath broke the silence. "Oh no," she said, her voice a whisper.

"We thought she had stopped to rest. It wasn't until we were almost to her side that we realized the gravity of the situation."

"Was she hurt?"

Porter stopped his story and looked up and down the aisle. It was easy for him to forget that he was talking to Emily in the middle of a large store.

"When we reached her, she was shivering so badly that she couldn't stop. We tried to talk to her, but her speech was slurred and she couldn't focus on any of our faces."

He shook his head to clear the images that were flooding back. "Emily, it was the scariest thing I had ever seen. Thomas picked her up and began running towards the house and I called 9-1-1 while racing after him."

Emily watched his face with wide eyes, clearly invested in the story. "What happened next?"

"My mom was already undressing Bree when I arrived. She wrapped her in warm blankets and put her in front of the fire but it wasn't enough. When they arrived, the paramedics took Bree to the hospital to bring her body temperature all the way back up."

Emily picked at a loose string on the pillow. "I guess I kind of know the ending since Bree is obviously very alive and well."

"True. But you asked me for a story about bravery. The brave part came when my brothers and I fessed up to our parents about what we had done. I expected my dad to shout and my mom to cry, but they did neither."

"What did they do?"

Porter shifted to the side, bringing his feet up to rest on the ottoman in front of him. "They forgave us."

Emily was silent for a moment. "You didn't get in any trouble?"

The weight of the memory pressed down on Porter's chest but he shook his head. "I was already a full-grown adult by that time. They didn't need to lecture me or my brothers. We knew how badly we had messed up."

Another memory tickled the back of Porter's mind, bringing a smile to his face. "That Christmas, Bree had so many presents under the tree that we got lectured for that. My parents said we were spoiling her and they were right. She's been wrapped around all of our fingers ever since that day."

"I think it is adorable that you spoil her."

An elderly couple walked down the aisle, stopping in front of the couches. It had been easy for Porter to forget where he was, but Emily pulled him to his feet. "We'll get out of your way," she said, moving to the side so the couple could look at the couches properly.

Disappointment flashed through his body, but Porter moved to the side. He didn't want to leave the bubble he and Emily were in.

"Thank you for sharing your story," Emily said. She rested her hand on his arm for the briefest of moments and every nerve in his body sang. Then she lowered her hand and began to walk towards the cash registers.

"I guess you've made up your mind?" Porter asked.

She flicked her ponytail to the side. "Well, the couch is for the center's waiting room. As far as I see it, we just had a great therapy session. Even without a llama to help."

Porter opened his mouth to respond but the retort died on his lips. She was right. There was something incredibly endearing about the woman who could get him to open up without trying.

* * *

By the time the couch was paid for and loaded, Porter's stomach was rumbling. He had been promised lunch if he helped and he knew just the place he wanted to show Emily. Around the corner from Cost Club was a small restaurant that served the best Mexican food in town. Visitors often passed right by it to head to one of the better-known chain restaurants in the area but locals knew and loved Mamma Salsa's cooking.

The inside of the restaurant smelled like a mix of fresh baked tortillas and grilled chicken. Porter watched Emily's face as she read the menu items. A server walked by with a burrito on a plate and Emily's eyes grew wide.

"Is every item on the menu that big?"

Porter laughed. "Pretty much. My family loves coming here because there is enough food for lunch one day and leftovers the next. They have a reputation for those gigantic burritos though."

"Remember, lunch is my treat since I commandeered your time and your truck." Emily planted her hands on her hips, staring him down as if challenging him to object.

"Whatever you say, boss." Porter ordered one of the burritos and smiled when Emily followed suit. They grabbed a small metal chili pepper stand with their order number and found an empty table in the back corner of the restaurant. The lunch rush was sure to bring in at least a couple of people Porter knew but he preferred to spend his time chatting with Emily and not an old friend.

Emily was telling Porter how she had come up with the name for her horse Maya when the bell above the door jangled and someone Porter recognized walked in. He tried to hide a smirk but Emily's eyes were too sharp.

"Who is that?" Emily asked.

The woman who entered had long blonde hair that was pulled back in a ponytail. She was a short 5 foot, 2 inch tall, but she could command a room. Porter leaned forward and lowered his voice to a whisper.

"That's Hazel. She's the town vet."

"I see." Emily watched Hazel walk to the counter, a small frown crossing her face. Porter didn't understand the change in her mood. Everyone in town was a fan of Hazel.

An idea crossed his mind that was just so ridiculous, he was tempted to shake it off. Could Emily be jealous? He needed to clear the air just to be sure.

Porter cupped a hand to the side of his mouth so no one but Emily could hear his whisper. "My brother Thomas has been nursing a crush on her for as long as I can remember. In fact, I won't be surprised if she becomes my sister-in-law one of these days."

That got a reaction. Emily looked back and forth between Hazel and Porter, her frown lifting to a smile. "She's pretty."

"Thomas sure thinks so." Hazel was pretty, but Emily was gorgeous. Hazel would make a great match for Thomas if Thomas ever got up the courage to pursue the relationship.

As they talked, Hazel made her way to their table. "Hello Porter," she said. She held her hand out to Emily. "I don't think we've met. I'm Hazel."

"I'm new to town. Emily Hutchings. It's nice to meet

you." The women shook hands and Porter crossed his fingers under the table. If he was lucky, maybe there'd be some double dates in the future with Thomas and Hazel tagging along. He hoped the women would be friends.

"I've been wanting you guys to meet," Porter said.

"Why is that?" Hazel asked.

"Emily has a herd of llamas. I'm guessing you don't work with too many of those guys around here."

Hazel held a hand up to her mouth. "I'd love to meet them if you're okay with that. I really don't get to treat many llamas but I have always loved them."

One point for the women getting along. Porter grinned.

"You're welcome to swing by any time." Emily pulled out her phone to swap info with Hazel.

Hazel turned her attention back to Porter. "How are things on the ranch?"

Porter hoped it was a veiled question. "Everyone's keeping busy. Thomas, especially, has had his hands full with the calving season."

A foot kicked him under the table. He glanced at Emily to see the subtle shake of her head.

Hazel's eyes brightened. "I've been keeping busy with all the births as well. Tell the family hi for me."

"Will do."

The server brought a bag of food to Hazel. She turned to Emily, all smiles. "It really was nice to meet you. I hope to see you again soon."

Porter got another soft kick to his leg when the door

closed behind Hazel. He held his hands out. "What was that for?"

"Subtle, much?" Emily asked. She began to laugh. "That poor woman. I wonder how often she gets hit on by her clients."

"I'm not sure, but as far as I know, she's still single. That means Thomas has a chance."

The words were out of his mouth before he realized how much he wanted the same chance with Emily. He said a silent prayer that both he and his brother would be able to find their way to love.

CHAPTER 10

Mornings were Emily's favorite time of the day. Her routine included light yoga to stretch her body and then a ten-minute meditation session to clear her mind. A minute into her meditation, she realized that going out with Porter was making it a little difficult to concentrate on anything other than the way she felt with him around. She pulled out her journal to read her entry from the night before.

I've never met someone who puts me at ease as much as Porter does. It doesn't seem to matter if we are working side by side or shopping. He has a gentle manner that makes me laugh and he's certainly easy on the eyes. It's way too early to be thinking about anything serious, but I can say that I like what I've seen so far.

Reading the section brought the same flutters to her stomach that had been there when she wrote the words. She didn't have years of history with Porter, but she could tell there was something special about the guy.

Emily was pulling on her boots when she got a text from Porter that she had left her sunglasses in his truck. He wanted to swing by sometime later in the day to drop them off. The thought of seeing him made the long work day ahead of her much more bearable.

By this point, Emily was getting overwhelmed with the amount of work she had left to do at the center. She would get one task accomplished and five more would pop up, demanding her attention. She was trying to focus on one job at a time to keep things more manageable. Her task for the day was painting which seemed a lot less enjoyable without Porter's help.

Emily drove to the ranch and started her rounds to see the animals. Stephen, as usual, was the first one to greet her. He nuzzled her cheek, checking to see that Emily was okay. This was why she kept pushing for the llama center. There was something special about working with the llamas. They had a unique ability to understand emotions. Eventually the city would understand and grant her the zoning change she needed.

Once the animals were taken care of, Emily headed inside. It didn't take long to put the final touches of paint in the first room and move to the second. In the beginning, there would only be a couple of therapists working but Emily had plans to expand to four offices. That meant a lot of painting up front, but less work when she was ready to expand.

She was belting out the lyrics to her music when there was a loud rapping on the door. With a sense of déjà vu, Emily ran to the bathroom to check her hair. She was not going to get caught off guard by Porter again. The knocking on the door was persistent. "I'm coming," she yelled. She walked to the door and flung it open. As she did, her hand flew to her mouth to stifle a gasp. There was a man standing on her porch. He was handsome and self-assured. He was not, however, Porter.

Emily lowered her hand to her stomach, swallowing a few times to avoid vomiting. "Gabe."

He pushed his hands through his golden hair; an action Emily had seen hundreds of times while they were dating.

"Hey Emmy. How's it going?"

Emily reached for the door frame, her legs shaking. "This. I." She took a deep breath to steady her voice while she straightened up. "Gabe, what are you doing here?"

It didn't seem possible that he would be able to surprise her further, but then he smiled. It sent a wave of nausea through Emily. The smile was meant to be reassuring, but all Emily could see was the manipulation behind it. He watched her with an intensity that made her squirm.

"Emmy. I was a jerk to you before."

Emily nodded, a chill washing over her body with the memory of the last time she saw him. This was the boyfriend who ditched her when things got hard, ignoring her phone calls when she was desperate for help. He walked away without a thought when she needed him the most.

"How did you find me?" Emily squeezed the door handle for stability while questions swirled through her mind.

"Your sister gave me the address. I'm here to make

things right." Gabe flashed her a lopsided grin. In the past, he'd smile and she'd forget everything he had done to hurt her. He was never overtly rude, but his slightly demeaning comments ate away at her day by day. He was the reason she almost gave up on the llama center.

"We broke up months ago. You made it very clear that you wanted nothing to do with me or my llamas."

His smile slipped. Gabe took a step towards her, his hand outstretched.

"Emmy, that is one of the biggest regrets of my life. I didn't realize how much I needed you. Can I take you out to lunch and we can talk?"

Emily looked down at her paint splattered hands. "I'm in the middle of a project right now. I can't just up and leave."

"Can I help you?" Gabe's eyes were sincere. Maybe he would finally answer some of her questions. It was worth giving him a chance.

For the second time that week, Emily found herself walking down the hallway of her new center with a handsome man following her. Walking with Porter had filled Emily's stomach with dancing butterflies. With Gabe, the butterflies were there but they were weighted down with heavy chains. Every time she'd glance back at him, the butterflies attempted to flap their wings but they couldn't break free.

Emily walked into the second bedroom and picked up her roller. "You can start over there," she said, pointing to a wall opposite of her. He needed to be as far away from her as possible. She waited until he picked up a paintbrush before trusting herself to speak. "Okay. What did you want to talk about?"

A heavy silence filled the room until Gabe found his words. "I didn't think I could handle the commitment of dating you but now I'd like to try."

"We haven't talked in months. What made you change your mind?" Emily focused on the paint roller, spreading paint up and down the wall so she wouldn't be tempted to look at his face.

"I miss you, Emmy." His voice was a whisper in her ear. Clearly, he hadn't understood the instructions to stay on his side of the room. Gabe rested his uncomfortably warm hands on her waist and Emily turned to face him.

Gabe trailed a finger down the side of her cheek, his touch making her stomach churn. "I thought I wanted to do something different with my life, but honestly, I'm miserable."

He was saying the right words. They were words she'd wanted to hear for months, and the pressure of his hands on her waist was familiar, but it no longer felt comfortable. Gabe tilted his chin down, his lips getting closer. He was closing his eyes and leaning in for the kiss when Emily pushed out of his arms. She took a step towards the center of the room.

"Gabe. We're not back together."

"But we could be." Gabe stepped towards her again, angling his head towards hers. Emily reached out her arm to stop him.

"Seriously? I am not kissing you right now. What is wrong with you?"

Gabe flinched backwards. "I drove all this way to see you."

"I didn't ask you to do that. You decided to make the drive without even asking me what I thought." Saying the words gave her courage. Gabe's attempts to kiss her reminded her of the many reasons why they had ultimately broken up. He always put more importance on what he wanted instead of listening to her.

Gabe stepped back. "You're right. I came here uninvited. Can I explain my side?" He grabbed his paintbrush and dipped it in the paint tray, moving it back and forth.

"You have five minutes." Emily glared at Gabe before she walked back to her wall. The feel of his hands around her waist lingered like a bad rash that she couldn't wipe off. Those hands had once felt safe, but now they felt weighted with expectation.

Porter's face pushed into Emily's mind. Even paint splattered and muddy from helping with the chores, he was the man whose hands she wanted to hold her. Not Gabe.

"Hey Emmy?"

Gabe's words broke through her daydreaming.

"Yeah?" She refused to turn around.

"What do I have to do to show you I'm serious? How do I win you back?"

Emily turned to face Gabe. She studied the face she had put years into loving. His eyes were filled with sincerity, but something was different. As Emily looked at the man she had given three years of her life to, she realized that the thing that had shifted was her. She was no longer willing to let her dreams be pushed to the side.

Gabe clearly wasn't going to help her get any work done effectively. Emily set her roller down and turned to face him. "I haven't changed my goals. This room we're painting? It's one of the offices for my llama therapy center."

Gabe shifted his feet and forced out a small chuckle. "You're still planning on doing that?"

"Of course, I am. Did you think I'd given up on my dreams?"

He paused before answering. "I don't know. Maybe." Gabe dipped his paintbrush in the tray again, swirling it in a circle.

Emily pointed to the door. "If you think that, then you don't really know me at all. You can show yourself out."

The look on Gabe's face was pure shock. He pulled the brush out of the paint tray and set it on a piece of plastic before crossing the room to Emily's side. She barely had time to fold her arms in front of her chest before he was standing next to her. He held his hand out but Emily refused to take it.

"Come on, Emmy. You know what I meant."

"I do? You never supported my dreams in the past and it sounds like that hasn't changed." A dull throbbing was beginning to pound at the base of her head. If she was lucky, she'd be able to finish working on one wall before the full-blown migraine hit.

Gabe placed his hand on her shoulder, and a fiery heat

flashed through her body. He needed to leave before she said something in anger that she couldn't take back.

His voice was low when he spoke again. "What I was trying to say is that I was hoping we could work on a new dream together. Maybe something that is more ... us?"

Gabe stretched his hands out again. Emily studied his face. He was still handsome as ever, but there was a giant wedge between them. He wrapped his arms around her waist and she shuddered. She had to get him out of the house before he tried to get any more physical with her.

"Gabe, I really need to do some work. Can we talk over dinner?" A restaurant would be a neutral location for her to dump him once and for all. Hopefully this time it would stick.

Gabe's brown eyes lit up. "Definitely. I'll pick you up at six."

There was a twinge in Emily's gut. He hadn't bothered to ask if the time worked for her but assumed he knew her answer.

"I think it would be better if I meet you there. I'll text you the address." Emily didn't want to be stranded if Gabe stormed out on her.

"I guess that works. I'll see you tonight."

"Thanks for your help," Emily said. She watched him walk away. It wasn't until he was almost to the door that Emily realized something. For all the "help" he had given, there wasn't a speck of paint anywhere on Gabe. All he had done was stand on the side of the room fiddling with a paintbrush.

She closed the door and leaned against it, her mind

automatically drifting to Porter and the afternoon he had spent with her. Was there really any point in comparing the two men? Porter's desire to help could be some ingrained cowboy thing and Gabe's lack of help the result of his upbringing, but it didn't really matter. Her choice between the two men was clear.

Maybe going out with Gabe was a bad idea, but she needed him to understand how serious she was about him leaving her alone. She had dreams to follow and work to do. There was room in her life for a man to be her partner, but it was painfully obvious that the man wasn't going to be Gabe.

Emily straightened her shoulders, the pounding in her head intensifying. If she didn't take some ibuprofen soon, her only date would be with her bed.

* * *

A FEW HOURS LATER, Emily set her paint roller in a bucket of water. The feeling of finishing the painting in the second office was liberating. Two rooms down, two to go. Paint flecks were swirling down the drain when Emily's phone chimed. She ignored the phone, taking the time to scrub her skin until no paint remained. Gabe would be disappointed if she showed up looking like she had actually been working. The thought of being judged bothered her, but Emily shook it off. The evening was about clearing Gabe from her life once and for all.

She checked her phone when she was dressed, expecting a confirmation text from Gabe. He never trusted that she'd be ready when she said she would. Instead of Gabe, there was a voicemail from Porter. Emily played the message twice, letting the sound of Porter's voice wash over her.

"Hey Emily. I was thinking about you all day today. How did the painting go? I wanted to stop by with your sunglasses but my brothers were teasing me for playing hooky yesterday so I was hoping I could bring them by later tonight. Anyway, say hi to Wembley for me."

The message was simple, but Emily's heart was touched. "He remembered Wembley," Emily whispered, tapping her fingers on the phone screen. She went to the dresser and pulled out a pair of pink flowered socks. It felt odd to be getting ready for a date with one man when all she could think about was a different one.

Emily reached for the phone. She was going to end things with Gabe, but that didn't mean she had to ignore Porter.

Porter was out of breath when he answered. "Hey Emily. What's up?"

"Did I catch you at a bad time?" Emily wished she had done a video call. She wanted to see what he was working on.

"Not really. I just finished giving Tiger his medicine. I swear, wrestling with this cat is harder than taking care of some of our bulls."

The image of Porter wrangling a small jungle animal made her smile. "So, the name fits the cat?"

"Definitely. He was so sweet when he was born. I'm not sure what happened."

Emily pulled on her shoes. "Maybe he's seen the way you paint. It turned him sour. Why are you drugging your cat?"

Porter's low chuckle sent a wave of longing through her.

"He got in a fight with some of the other cats on the ranch and cut his ear. We don't want it getting infected. That's ranch life for you."

"I'd like to meet your feisty Tiger. He sounds awesome." Emily clamped a hand over her mouth. Was she really inviting herself over to the ranch?

Porter cleared his throat. "Well, that's kind of why I called. I was hoping I could take you out again sometime. I don't have any furniture I need to buy but I think it's my turn to pay for dinner."

Emily's breath hitched in her throat. "I'd like that."

"Me too. Is tonight too soon to ask to see you?"

A wave of regret pressed down on her heart. "I wish I could, but I already have other plans." They were stupid plans that she wasn't looking forward to, but at least they had a purpose. She was clearing the way so her heart was totally free next time she went out with Porter.

"Some other time?"

"Definitely. Can I call you tomorrow?" Emily held her breath, hoping he'd say yes.

"I'll keep my ringer on. Enjoy your evening, Emily."

"Goodbye, Porter." Emily hung up the phone and smoothed down her hair. She took a final glance in the mirror to check her outfit, but it didn't really matter how she looked. The man she really wanted to be seeing was the man who wore a cowboy hat, not a baseball jersey.

When the doorbell rang a half hour later, Emily was ready. It was time to end the non-existent relationship with Gabe once and for all. Hopefully this time he would respect her decision.

CHAPTER 11

Thunder was rumbling outside when Porter hung up the phone with Emily. Seconds later, the clouds opened and rain pounded against the window panes. Porter's body tensed. He did not need to deal with a flash flood anywhere else on the ranch. The basement had been enough.

When he ran into the house his family was waiting, their faces turned towards him. So much for making a private call.

"Did you ask her out?" Hudson asked.

"I did." He knew everyone wanted to hear what her answer was, but Porter was having fun messing with his family. He hung his hat by the door, letting the silence stretch out.

Reid finally spoke up. "Hey. Don't keep us waiting. What did she say?"

"She has other plans." Porter waited for the muttering of his siblings to die down.

Mom looked up from the couch where she was knitting a red and blue striped scarf. "Are you okay with that?"

"I guess so." He looked out the window, hunching his shoulders before he let out a loud, dejected sigh. Teasing them was far too easy. When Hope placed her hand on his back he straightened up with a laugh. "I'm kidding. She said she'd call me tomorrow."

Thomas jumped off the couch and smacked Porter's shoulder. "You could have led with that."

"Yeah, but leaving you in suspense is far more fun." Porter plopped down in an armchair that had seen more than its fair share of wrestling matches. The fabric on the arms was wearing thin from years of kids playing on it. He crossed his arms in front of him and looked at the family.

"It's the last day for the college kids before they head back, right?" Porter asked.

"Right," Hope said. "Hudson and I need to head out early tomorrow morning so I'm awake for class on Monday."

There was still a bright spot to the evening. Porter smiled. "I don't have a date tonight but I could sure go for some ice cream at that new shop downtown. It can be your going away party."

"I'm down," Hope said.

Thomas raised his eyebrows. "Ice cream in this weather?"

Porter nodded. "Maybe it won't be so busy there."

Mom Matthews unraveled a section of blue yarn. "I think it's a great idea. Dinner will be ready in a half hour, and then we can go."

Porter patted the arm of the chair he was in before standing. He needed to check the chicken coop to make sure the door was still open. The last storm, wind had blown the door closed, which led to a bunch of unhappy chickens scattered all over the ranch. They were most likely heading home to roost in this bad weather. He was walking towards the back door when Wyatt ran into the room, his face flushed.

"I need help, guys."

All eyes turned to Wyatt.

"What happened?" Porter asked.

"The cattle spooked. I was moving a group of them to the far field when a huge clap of thunder startled them. Last I saw, they were making a beeline for the Landon property line."

Porter groaned. If they got into the hay fields, they could cause a lot of damage. Strained neighbor relations were the last thing he needed. He pointed to Thomas. "You take the east trail. Reid, you take the west."

"What about me?" Wyatt asked.

"You can follow me on the ATV. We'll go down the middle. Hopefully we can head them off before they cause too much trouble."

Porter pulled on his rain boots and ran to the ATV with Wyatt close behind. They watched Thomas and Reid take off and then they left, splashing through mud puddles while rain poured from the sky.

The rain was coming down in sideways sheets when Porter and Wyatt found the cattle huddled together at the bottom of a hill. He radioed his siblings to come help herd them back to the ranch. As the cattle headed back to the ranch it quickly became apparent that all the cows weren't okay. One of the larger cows was limping. She followed after the herd with a strained gait.

Porter and Thomas separated her from the herd when they got to the pasture where Hope and Bree were waiting. Hope talked to the cow, patting her back while Thomas examined her leg.

"She has a large gash," he said.

"We should probably call the vet," Hope said. "She's bleeding a lot."

"It's shallow," Thomas said. "I'll put a bandage on the cut and call Hazel in the morning if it looks bad."

Porter bit back a smile. He was surprised Thomas wasn't calling Hazel right away, but he knew better than to pry. Thomas had experienced similar problems to his when it came to dating women.

Dating a cowboy looked great in the movies, with their spotless shirts and long, romantic evenings under the stars. In reality, working a ranch was nothing like the movies. Emergencies cropped up at all hours of the day and night. Porter couldn't tell the ranch to slow down while he planned romantic outings any more than he could tell the rain to come at a more convenient time.

Dinner was waiting on the table when the family came in from the rain. Mom set down a bowl of salad next to the pan of piping hot lasagna. "Did you find them all?"

Porter rubbed a hand through his hair. "Neighbor relations are safe. They stopped right outside the Landon property line."

"One of the cows is hurt though," Thomas said.

"Is it bad?" Mom asked.

"Thomas hopes so," Bree said.

"Why would you say that?" Thomas asked. "I don't want any of our animals to be hurt."

"Oh, please. We've all seen the way you watch Hazel when you are near her."

Porter clamped a hand down on Thomas's shoulder. "Let it go. She's trying to rile you up." He kept the pressure until Thomas visibly relaxed and sank into a chair.

"Maybe you're right," Thomas said. "Anyway, I think she will probably be fine. I'll have Hazel check the cut if it doesn't look like it's healing properly."

"Fingers crossed that she's fine," Hope said.

Porter sat in his chair and reached for the salad tongs. "Dinner looks great, Mom."

A chorus of thank you's rang around the table before the conversation took the normal turn. Laughter was punctuated by exaggerated hand gestures, the scraping of forks on plates, and an occasional belch. Porter appreciated having a full house for the evening, although part of him was ready to send half the family back to school. Extra bodies meant extra help, but also a lot of mental energy worrying if everyone was doing okay.

* * *

AFTER A BRIEF SCUFFLE TO determine who was driving, the family headed out to their cars. Bree waved her keys in the air. "This way to the fun car."

"Shotgun," Porter called, running past Hudson to take the door handle. Bree had been an officially licensed driver for just over a month. She was a fairly safe driver, but her sense of direction was awful. Porter wanted to make sure they made it to the proper destination.

By the time they arrived at the ice cream shop, Porter felt like he was going crazy. They had passed three trucks that looked like Emily's on the way to the shop, and each one made his heart speed up a notch. The thought of seeing Emily's face sent a flutter of longing through him that he hadn't felt in years.

Bree parked the car across the way from yet another Emily truck look-alike. This sent Porter's heart thumping again. He sat in the car for just a moment longer than his siblings and took a couple of steadying breaths to bring his mind back to his family. Then he climbed out and headed for the shop door.

The siblings were spoon deep in a ten-scoop ice cream sundae when there was a commotion outside. Porter glanced out the window, watching with interest as a group of teenagers ran by. They were followed by a woman with dirty-blonde hair. Porter lowered his spoon and leaned forward to see if it was Emily. When he sat back, Finn was watching him.

"You okay, brother?"

Porter rubbed his forehead. "I'm good. I thought I saw someone I knew." He reached across the bowl for a spoonful of the brookie dough, making sure to get a piece of brownie and cookie in the bite. No one needed to know just how much he was daydreaming about Emily.

By the time they were finished with the giant sundae, Porter had stopped glancing at every woman who walked past the window who happened to have hair the same color as Emily's. Porter pushed back his chair and stood. "Everyone ready to go?" he asked.

The rowdy crew nodded yes and headed to the cars, their chatter filling the air. Wyatt let out a loud whoop and people all around them stopped to stare. Porter lifted his hand in an apologetic wave only to lower it when he recognized a pair of blue eyes studying him from the restaurant across the street.

It was Emily, and she wasn't alone. The man standing next to her looked displeased to have been interrupted. Porter lowered his hand, keeping eye contact with the woman he had been fantasizing about moments before. She hadn't given him a reason for why she couldn't go out, but the answer was pretty clear seeing the man standing next to her. From the looks of things, she was already on a date. They were nowhere close to exclusive, but Porter felt like he was getting punched in the gut.

Porter started to look away but then the man draped an arm across Emily's shoulders and jealousy surged to the surface. Emily wasn't just comfortable with the man. It looked like she was in a relationship with him. Flames coursed through Porter's body when the man bent over to place a kiss on Emily's cheek. He knew he should turn away from the scene but he was glued to the spot.

When Emily shrugged the man's arm off of her shoulders, Porter took an involuntary step forward. The man tried to drape his arm around Emily's shoulders once more and she shook his arm off, turning to glare at him. As she did so, something inside Porter snapped.

Emily may have ditched him to go out with another guy, but there was no way Porter was going to watch a man mistreat a woman in front of him. Emily deserved better.

He was halfway across the street when the man leaned down and kissed Emily on the lips. He was two-thirds of the way across the street when Emily lifted her hand. The crack of her hand against the man's cheek stilled all nearby conversations. A voice in Porter's mind warned him to back up but he was already too close to Emily.

"Hi Emily. Need any help?" he asked.

The man stepped forward, puffing out his chest. Porter sized him up. Emily's date was taller, but Porter was pretty sure he could take him in a fight. Especially when he realized that Thomas and Reid were flanking him.

Emily's eyes were shooting daggers at the men. "I'm fine, Porter. No one asked for you to come over here."

"You didn't look fine from over there." Porter took another step towards the man.

"What's your problem?" the man asked.

"My problem is that your hands seem to be all over Emily, and it doesn't look like she appreciates it much."

"That's not what she said when I kissed her in the past."

Porter lunged forward, the pressure on his shirt keeping him inches from the man's face. He could feel his brothers trying to tug him back, but he wasn't going to leave until the jerk who was harassing Emily was gone.

"Yeah. I'm not sure what your relationship was in the past, but you'd better leave her alone today."

Emily pushed the men apart. "Gabe, it's time for you to go."

Porter waited for Gabe to leave. Then he turned to Emily. He was expecting gratitude but fire was still in her eyes.

"I didn't ask for your help," she said.

"Sorry. It looked like you were in trouble." Porter tucked his thumbs in his back pockets and tried to smile.

"And you think that I wanted you to save me? What were you going to do? Punch Gabe?" Emily stabbed him in the chest with each question, pushing him further away with each poke. "I didn't ask for you to come save me and I certainly didn't need it." She pulled out her keys and stomped over to her truck, pulling the door open. "I can take care of myself," she said. Then she slammed the door shut and backed out onto the street.

A heavy silence pressed down on the brothers. Porter looked back and forth from Thomas to Reid. "I guess I stepped in it this time."

"I haven't seen you this protective of a woman since, well, Cassidy," Thomas said.

Porter ran a hand through his hair. "I don't know what came over me. I saw that Gabe guy pressing himself on her and I snapped."

"Yeah," Reid said. "That's why we're here. I half expected you to level the guy. I'm guessing this is the infamous Emily?"

Porter nodded. "It doesn't matter now. I don't think she wants to talk to me ever again."

Thomas patted Porter's shoulder. "You never know

what will happen tomorrow. Maybe she'll forget all about it."

"Wishful thinking," Porter said. He took a deep breath and followed his brothers back to the cars where the rest of the family was waiting.

"I don't want to talk about it," Porter said, anticipating the barrage of questions that was sure to come.

Mom Matthews raised an eyebrow but said nothing as she climbed into Hope's car. Porter folded himself into the front seat of Bree's car and braced himself for the lecture that was sure to come.

"That's Emily?" Bree asked.

"Yep," Porter said.

"Who's the guy?"

"I'm guessing her ex. I don't know," Porter said.

"Huh." Bree pulled onto the street, pausing at the first stop sign to change the channel on the radio. "Sucks to be him," she said. Then she cranked the radio up and started to sing.

Porter leaned back against the headrest, grateful that the inquisition was over for the moment. When they got home, Porter pulled on his work boots.

"I'll be in in a sec," he said. "I want to check on the injured cow." He was partway to the pasture when he heard footsteps behind him. Thomas jogged to Porter's side.

"I want to see how she's doing, too," Thomas said.

When they reached the cattle, it was clear that the cow was still in pain. She held her hoof above the ground, limping around on three legs.

"Do you think we'll need to get her checked tomorrow?" Porter asked.

"I'm not sure," Thomas said. He rubbed the cow's back. "If we do, I think Hazel will be a big help." He rocked back and forth, a question clearly on his mind.

"What's up, Thomas?" Porter said. "You can ask. If it's about Emily, I'm really fine."

"It's not that," Thomas said. "I was just wondering how you would feel if I started dating again."

Porter leaned back against the fence, studying his brother's face. "Does it really matter what I think? For the record, I think it would be awesome."

Thomas jammed his thumbs through his belt buckles. "I guess it doesn't really matter. I just always assumed you'd be married first again. When I picked you up from Emily's ranch, I thought you had maybe found someone worth pursuing, but now I'm not so sure. I don't want you to feel bad if someone beats you to the punch."

Porter clamped his hands down on Thomas's shoulders. "If you have someone you are interested in, go for it. This family could use some good news."

He hoped his encouraging words would mask the serious depression he felt knowing that Emily may never want to speak to him again. If he couldn't have his happy ending, at least his brother could.

Porter followed Thomas back to the house. "Let me know how it goes with Hazel," he said. He waited until he was alone in his room before he bowed his head to say a silent prayer. *Lord, if it be thy will, please help Thomas with Hazel. He's even better than I am at sticking his nose where it doesn't belong.*

CHAPTER 12

After the tumultuous evening the night before, Porter volunteered to drive the twins to the airport. They talked non-stop all the way there, but the quiet drive home gave him plenty of time to think. He had messed up with Emily, and he needed a way to fix it. He was sitting in the driveway with his head leaned back against the seat when the passenger's side door flung open. Thomas climbed in and sat down, looking at Porter expectantly.

"What's up, Thomas?" Porter asked. He sat up straight, turning towards his brother. "I got everyone off safely."

"I might have ruined something." Thomas turned his hat over in his hands. "I need help."

Porter's stomach sank. Messing up on the ranch meant more work for everyone, and they were already stretched thin. "What did you do?"

Thomas turned his hat over a couple more times. "It's

Hazel. I tried to ask her out, but the words got stuck somewhere in my throat and I couldn't say them."

Porter knew that feeling well. He had gotten the courage to ask Emily out and all it had gotten him was trouble. She wasn't returning his text messages and he was pretty sure he knew why. He hadn't minded his own business.

"Women," he said. "I don't know if I'll ever figure them out. How about you tell me exactly what happened and I'll see if there's anything we can do to fix it."

He leaned back against the headrest once more and listened to Thomas talking. Maybe helping his brother would help him figure out what to do about Emily.

Thomas told him about awkwardly asking Hazel to come check the cow and then trying to turn it into a date. Porter sat up straight. "Wait. She's coming back to the ranch and that has you stressed out? I'd give anything for Emily to come to the ranch. I'd even take a phone call at this point. You've got nothing to worry about."

"Are you sure? I really like her." Thomas drummed his fingers on the dashboard. "I don't want to mess this one up."

Porter clamped a hand down on Thomas's shoulder. "You're going to be just fine. Think of something you'd like to do with Hazel and then you'll know what to ask her."

Thomas nodded and reached for the door handle. "Thanks, Port. What about Emily? What are you going to do about her?"

That was the million-dollar question. Porter shrugged. "I wish I knew."

* * *

A WEEK LATER, Emily still wasn't answering his phone calls. Porter was on his way home from the feed store when he made a snap decision. Instead of turning onto Old Ranch Road, he flipped his car around and headed to Emily's llama ranch. When he pulled down the driveway, two pairs of eyes peered over the edge of the fence at him. He wasn't sure, but he guessed it was Stephen and Wren.

The house looked different when Porter pulled up to the front. It took him a moment to realize that the door had been painted a bright turquoise blue. Maybe Emily had been so busy painting, she didn't have time to answer calls. He headed up the steps with the memory of the last time he had visited filling his mind. How had he gone from being friends with Emily to being shut out completely? It didn't make sense.

Porter rapped his knuckles on the door, his mouth suddenly dry. Emily's truck was out front, but there was no movement inside. He knocked again, calling out her name. It was one thing to ignore text messages and phone calls. It was another thing entirely to ignore a person standing on the porch.

As the silence stretched on, Porter craned his neck to look through the side windows. Emily's purse was inside, but there was no other movement. She was definitely ignoring him. Porter reached for the handle. If she wasn't going to come out, he was going to go in.

He was turning the knob when he heard a voice

shouting behind him. Porter spun around, sticking his hands in his back pockets so he didn't look guilty.

Emily was crossing the driveway. Porter stepped off the porch, taking a few steps towards her.

"I like the new door," he said, gesturing towards it .

"What are you doing here?" Emily asked. There was no warmth in her voice.

"I wanted to talk." Porter planted his feet. He wasn't going anywhere until he had some answers.

If the frown on Emily's face dropped any lower, it would scrape across the ground. She planted her hands on her hips. "Porter, I'm a busy woman. I don't have time to talk right now."

"Yeah. You didn't have time on any of the days I called you, either." He was on a roll, the words spilling out. "We were friends last week, and today you can barely look at my face. Why?"

"Do I really have to spell it out for you? I don't have the energy to spend on hot heads who pick fights."

Porter rocked back on his heels, her words punching him more effectively than fists. "That's not fair. I was trying to defend you."

"From what?"

"From that guy." Porter couldn't grasp why Emily was being so unreasonable. The man had clearly been pushing his boundaries. "You don't even know who he is or what the situation was." Emily took a step forward, pushing him back with her finger. "I didn't ask for your help and I didn't need it."

Porter flinched and began to step backwards until his

foot hit the bottom step. There wasn't anywhere else for him to go unless he walked back up to the door. He held up his hands, his mind racing. If there was a solution, he'd better think of it quickly or he was going to be trying to pull his boots out of this mess for a long time.

Although the cowboy hated backing down from any fight, he could see Emily's point. Or at least he could pretend like he saw it.

"Okay, okay." He whipped off his hat and held it against his chest. "Cowboy's honor. I'm sorry. I thought that guy was pushing himself on you and I kind of snapped."

Emily's hands didn't leave her hips, but a smirk lifted the side of her mouth. Porter pretended like he was a statue while Emily glared at him. Then her hands slowly lowered.

"Gabe is my ex-boyfriend. One of the main reasons I broke up with him is because of his aggressiveness. He never really cared what I wanted or thought unless it aligned perfectly with his needs."

"I should have let you handle him." Porter felt genuinely sorry. His mom worked hard to raise independent daughters who didn't need a man to defend them, and yet at the first sight of a woman in distress, Porter lost his mind. He could see the value of an independent woman, but could he respect that?

The tension in the air was ebbing, but Porter couldn't relax. Not until he knew that Emily had forgiven him. He watched her face, waiting for her expression to smooth out. After what felt like an eternity, a true smile crossed her lips.

"You're right. You should have let me handle it." She started to laugh. "But did you see his face when you got close? I think you scared Gabe badly enough that he won't be back any time soon."

Was this a test to see if Porter agreed with Emily? "I'm glad he's gone, if that's what you want. I know it's none of my business, but what were you doing at dinner with the guy if you clearly don't like him anymore?"

The guarded look was back on Emily's face. She looked towards the barns and said nothing.

Porter stepped to her side. "Never mind. Like I said, it's none of my business." Even though it wasn't his business, he couldn't help but pry. He wanted to know everything there was to know about Emily. The mere act of standing close to her sped up his heartbeat so he could feel it thumping out of his chest.

Emily muttered something under her breath and then she plopped down on one of the steps. Porter hesitated for just a moment before joining her.

"Can you handle the truth?" she asked. Something in her voice was small and broken, and Porter wanted to scoop her in his arms and make it better. She didn't like help though, which was the entire point of their tension from earlier.

"Always," Porter said.

The wind that had been whipping past slowed to a small breeze as if it was wanting to hear the story as well. Porter turned his knees towards hers, rubbing a fraying spot on his jeans so he wouldn't be tempted to reach out.

When Emily began to speak, the words were low. "I

didn't know what kind of a guy Gabe was until we had been dating for a while. In the beginning, he wasn't so controlling. In fact, he was charming and good natured. We worked very well together."

She bit the side of her cheek. "I don't know when things began to shift, but I remember the day when I realized things weren't all sunny and happy. I had been telling Gabe about my dreams for opening the llama therapy center and he stood up and walked out of the room. I figured he had forgotten something in the kitchen, but then the door slammed shut and he didn't come back."

Emily closed her eyes and took a few deep breaths.

"How long was he gone?" Porter clasped his hands together tightly, reminding them to not push Emily's boundaries.

"We didn't speak for three days. At first, I assumed he was dumping me for good, but then he came back, acting like nothing had happened." Emily folded her arms in front of her, resting them on her legs. "That should have been my cue to exit, but by that time we had already been dating for a year and a half. I figured it was a fluke and I forgave him."

"Did things get better?" Porter wasn't sure how much he could pry, but Emily was talking to him and he didn't want her to stop.

"They did, for a while. As long as I didn't bring up anything about the llama center or my dreams, things were fine. In fact, Gabe started repairing a vintage car and that kept him entertained for hours." She looked towards the barn again.

"I'm guessing you're not a fan of vintage cars?" Porter was trying to be objective but it didn't seem like any of Emily's needs were getting met.

"I was happy that he was happy, but every night when I'd go home after hanging out with Gabe, I'd realize that the day had been completely focused on him. None of the conversations were ever about me or our future together."

Emily was staring into the distance, lost in thought. Porter tried to see things from Gabe's side. There must have been some reason behind his actions but he couldn't see any. The more he thought about it, the angrier he got. Emily deserved so much better.

"When did you finally break up with him?"

Emily shifted on the step. "You'd think I'd say right away, but it took me another year to finally split from him. Every time I'd think I'd had enough; he would change just enough to lure me back in. That's why he came here last week."

"Huh," Porter said. Now that he knew the whole story, he was thinking about how nice it would have felt to land his fist on Gabe's jaw. He guessed that would have made things much worse with Emily though.

"When you saw us outside that restaurant?" Emily tucked her hair behind her ear.

"Yeah?"

"We had gone there so I could end things with him in a safe space. I was hoping this time it would stick."

Anger surged through Porter at the thought of her needing a safe space. "Did he hurt you?" If the answer was yes, Porter was going to have some more apologizing to do because Gabe would definitely be getting that punch to the face.

Emily placed her hand on his arm. "No. He never physically hurt me. His words sometimes hurt, but that's something we're pretty good at doing to each other as humans in general."

"I'm confused. What did you need protection from?" It was taking a lot of Porter's concentration to stay focused on Emily's words and not his desire to clobber Gabe.

"I figured if we were somewhere public, he wouldn't cause a scene." Emily glanced towards Porter and then turned away. He thought he could see a bit of a smile. Her words thudded into his chest.

"And then this big doofus came over and did exactly what you were trying to avoid. Someone should talk to that guy." He bumped his shoulder against hers. This time when she looked at him a smile was definitely dancing across her lips.

"Uh huh. So, what do you have to say for yourself?"

Porter hesitated for just a moment before he reached for Emily's hand. "I already said I was sorry, but now that I know the story, I'm even more sorry. I usually behave pretty well in public."

"I'd have to see that to believe it." Emily scooted close enough to Porter that he could smell the floral shampoo she used.

He wrapped his arm around her shoulders. He could get used to holding her close every day. "Does that mean you might actually go to dinner with me sometime?"

Emily nudged his knee with hers. "How does Friday night sound?"

Relief shot through Porter's body. He hadn't completely ruined things. "I think I can make that work. There will be no ex-boyfriends around, right?"

Emily's laughter lit her eyes. "Not that I know of. And no ex-girlfriends?"

"Not a chance." Porter gave Emily's shoulder a little squeeze before he pushed himself off the steps. "I'd better be getting back to the ranch with the chicken feed. Thanks for giving me another chance."

Emily followed him to his car. He was climbing into the front seat when she stopped him. "Oh Porter?" she asked.

"Yes?" He liked the way his name sounded coming from her lips.

"On Friday it's your turn." She placed her hands on her hips.

"My turn for what?" Did she need him to apologize again? That was something he was willing to do for as long as it took for her to believe him.

"It's your turn to tell me about your ex-girlfriends. I assume you have at least one or two?"

The words thudded against his heart, making it hard to keep the smile on his face. "I guess you'll have to wait and see." Porter slid the truck into reverse and backed out of the driveway. He kept the smile plastered on his face until he was safely away from Emily's ranch. Then the smile fell.

He wanted Emily to know about his past, but how was he supposed to tell her that he was a widower? People always acted strange when they heard about Cassidy and the baby. Porter didn't want to spook her before their relationship had time to form roots. He also didn't want to lie.

Questions swirled through his mind the closer he got to home but he pushed them to the back of his mind. That was a Friday problem, and he had a whole slew of Monday problems to deal with instead.

CHAPTER 13

Emily watched Porter's truck pull away. The tires were disappearing around the corner when she realized how much she had been talking. Her stomach sank. She was pretty sure there was some advice somewhere about not talking about the ex-boyfriend until later in the relationship. If Porter actually showed up for their date on Friday, she'd be thrilled.

Emily's job for the day was clearing the muck out of one of the unused stalls on the ranch. The previous owners had built a section of stalls on the far end of the property. She wasn't sure what their purpose had been, but she didn't want the llamas wandering into them until she could properly inspect the ground to make sure there weren't rusty nails littering the place.

She was foot deep in loosened dirt when her phone began to ring. Emily tapped her ear buds to answer. "Hey Kayla. What's up?"

Kayla's excited voice filled the phone. "So, Mom just

called. They are doing a surprise party for Grandpa's 80th birthday this weekend. Did she call you?"

"Not yet. Tell me the details." If anyone deserved a special party, it was their grandpa.

Kayla took a breath and dived in. "The party is on Sunday. You know how Grandma loved family dinners, right? Well, Grandpa thinks we are hosting a regular Sunday dinner but more and more people heard about it and want to come. It's a way to honor her memory while celebrating him."

Emily's stomach sank listening to Kayla's words. Sure, it was easy for all the families that lived nearby to gather. It was a little more complicated for Emily when she lived in another state.

Kayla was still jabbering on. "You're going to be there, right? Please say you can make it."

Emily pushed her hair off her face. "Kayla, you know how much I idolize Grandpa. I'd be there in a heartbeat if I could but I don't know how to make that happen."

"I checked the flights. You could fly here early Sunday morning and be back on Monday afternoon."

"That would work great if I didn't have a ranch full of animals to take care of." Emily's mind was shuffling through all the possibilities. She could leave extra food and water, but the idea of leaving the llamas even for a day didn't sit well with her. Not when they were still adjusting to the ranch like she was.

"Can't you find someone to check on them? Some neighbor kid would probably be thrilled to make a bit of extra cash."

She was trying to be helpful, but Kayla didn't understand what Emily was working with. These weren't small animals like cats or dogs that almost anyone could play with. "It's not that simple, sis."

Kayla huffed into the phone. "Just promise me you'll try."

Emily was about to say no when something clicked. She happened to know the perfect cowboy to ask for a recommendation. If there was a ranch babysitting service, Porter would have the name.

"No promises, but I'll see what I can do."

* * *

BY THE TIME Friday rolled around, Emily's stomach was tied in knots. She happened to be looking out the window when Porter arrived for her date. He didn't need to know that she had been hovering between an oversized armchair and a spot by the front curtains, trying to calm her nerves. When he climbed out of the truck, her jaw dropped.

Porter was wearing a pale blue button-down shirt with the sleeves pushed partway up. The fabric was just thin enough to hint at the muscles beneath, but that wasn't what held her attention. A gigantic belt buckle was sitting front and center of Porter's outfit; two golden calves with their horns locked in an epic battle of some sort. Even from the window she could make out the details.

She didn't care if he caught her spying. Emily pulled her door open and went to greet him on the steps.

"Emily!" Porter stepped quickly to her side, holding out his arm. "You look beautiful."

She took the arm, confirming that yes, there were plenty of muscles hiding beneath that shirt. "Thanks. And you look . . ." The compliment died on her lips. What could she say? He was as handsome as ever, but the belt buckle was something else entirely.

"Creative," she finally said. "You look . . . creative."

Porter grinned and pointed to the buckle. "Thanks. Isn't this a beauty?"

"It's certainly something." Emily let Porter lead her to the side of the truck. He opened the door and she slid into the seat, completely at a loss for words.

Porter jogged to the other side of the truck and climbed in. "Where to?"

"I thought you were taking me out," Emily said. "That means you pick where we go."

"I know just the place." Porter put the truck in gear and backed onto the street. "You're going to love it."

They were driving down Main Street when Porter smacked the steering wheel. "You're pretty new to the town still, right?"

Emily nodded.

"Have you been able to explore things much?"

"Not really. I haven't been anywhere but the hardware store, the grocery store, and the feed store."

Porter glanced her way, his eyebrows raised. "It's official. I'm giving you the Matthew's family tour."

He pulled to a stop beside an old brick building. Reddish-brown bricks formed walls that looked like they were about to fall down. "This building here is where I went to church the first fifteen years of my life."

"It's beautiful." Emily appreciated the old architecture.

"It really is. The city was going to knock it down but my family helped raise the funds to retrofit the building. I baked so many cupcakes that summer, I still can't stand the taste of them."

The thought of a younger Porter selling cupcakes warmed her heart. He was probably irresistible.

Porter pointed to the other side of the street where a more modern building sat, the open paned windows a stark contrast to the heavy brick. The sidewalk in front of the building wound past a sculpture of a man riding a horse, ending at tall glass doors.

"Here you have the town library."

"Do people even use libraries anymore?" Emily couldn't even remember the last time she had stepped in one.

In response, Porter drove around to the back of the building where there was a pavilion nestled among numerous tall trees. "I know a lot of people read online now, but there is still a huge demand for print books. This is the heart of our town. You can find an event here almost every weekend. In fact, if we're lucky, we may catch part of a concert on our way home."

"I can't imagine Elk Mountain pulling in too many people for a concert."

Porter laughed. "You'd be surprised. In another hour the street will be lined with vendors pushing carts. My favorite is the cinnamon almond cart."

Emily's stomach growled in response. She clutched her hand to her stomach but the damage was done.

Porter drummed his fingers on the steering wheel. "I can take the hint. I'm heading to the restaurant now."

The rest of the buildings passed by quickly. Emily wanted to hear more of the Matthew's family tour, but Porter was focused on the road ahead. Before long he pulled into the parking lot of a small restaurant. The blue and white striped canopy out front didn't give any hint to what kind of food was inside.

Porter parked the car and then put his hand on Emily's knee, sending her pulse into overdrive. "Wait there," he said.

She took a deep breath to slow her heart rate. Porter opened the door and held his hand out to help her down. Somehow, between the tour guide and the rumbling stomach, Emily had forgotten about Porter's belt buckle. Impossibly, it appeared to have grown in size during the drive.

They took a couple of steps towards the restaurant and Porter stopped, bending over double.

"Are you okay?" Emily asked. She placed a hand on his back, rubbing it in a slow circle. He straightened up and Emily could see his giant grin.

"Everything is fine. You just earned me twenty bucks." Porter turned back to the truck and flung the door open.

"I'm confused," Emily said. She followed behind him.

"My brother Reid bet me twenty bucks that you'd say something about this belt buckle. He was convinced you wouldn't let me out of the truck with it on."

Emily tried to word her response with tact. "It is

certainly an interesting style, but I'm not going to tell anyone what to wear."

"That's what I told Reid." Porter unhooked a clasp on either side of the belt buckle and removed it, letting it dangle from one finger before he tossed it into the cab. "Isn't it something?"

"Where on earth did you get it?" Emily was laughing now, the prank putting her at ease. If Porter was comfortable enough to tease her, the evening was off to a good start.

"Reid won it at the county fair when he was nine. I still remember him wearing it to school with a grin on his face. When he came home, he threw the belt in the corner. I was sure the kids had been teasing him. Thomas and I were ready to defend his honor until we got the whole story. Apparently, it was such a big hit with the kids that the teacher asked him to please leave it home next time so the class could do their work." Porter reached for the buckle. "I can put it back on if you want some extra attention on our date."

Emily pushed his arm back towards the truck. "I'm not sure I can handle that sort of attention. Let's keep things a little more low key." Porter certainly didn't need an obnoxious belt to draw attention to himself. His dark hair and earnest eyes were enough to make any woman swoon. Emily didn't want to share him with anyone else.

Porter grinned and tossed the belt buckle to the seat of the truck once more. "Next time." He held his arm out for Emily and together they walked into the restaurant.

Speakers overhead were playing a country song that

Emily didn't recognize. She was so focused on the song; she didn't notice when Porter tugged her hand.

"They've got our seat," he said.

Emily nodded. "Sorry. I was trying to figure out who sings this song."

Porter glanced at the hostess. "Should we let her in on the secret?"

"Not yet," the hostess said. "I like to give people a minute to figure it out. Your waitress will be with you soon." She handed them two menus and walked off.

The thought of a mystery to solve set Emily's mind racing. If it was an obscure artist Emily probably wouldn't be able to guess, but she wasn't going to go down without a fight.

"Dolly Parton, early years?" she guessed as she slid into her chair.

Porter shook his head, his handsome eyes crinkling around the edges. "Good guess, but no. This restaurant plays music from our local musicians. It's their way to support the community."

"That's really sweet. So, have you recorded any songs for them? I'm sure your gospel hip hop would be a hit."

Porter winked. "I'm letting my music career stay on the back burner for a while. My sister Hope recorded a few songs a while back. I think they are out of the rotation by now though."

The waitress approached, carrying two tall glasses of water. "Hi there, folks. Welcome to The Spotted Cow. Are we celebrating anything today?"

It was Emily's turn to tease Porter. She placed a hand

over his. "He finally got the courage to tell his parents about us eloping. They disowned him, but now we can live our truth." Porter's hand was warm beneath hers. He covered her hand with his other one. Emily belatedly realized the heat blasting through her body had a little to do with the forwardness of her joke and a lot to do with the calloused hands that enveloped hers, giving them a gentle squeeze.

When Porter pulled his hands away and stood up, Emily's heart sank. She had taken the joke too far. He walked over to her side of the table, dragging a chair behind him. Then, without looking at her face once, he plopped the chair down right beside her and sat, putting his arm around her shoulders. She hesitated for a second and then leaned in close, appreciating the tingles that raced through her body. He smelled incredible.

"Yep. As you can see, we're two lovebirds who finally came clean to the family." As Porter spoke, he squeezed her arm. Emily was sure the entire restaurant could hear her heart thumping out of her chest.

The waitress looked back and forth between Emily and Porter. Then she held her hand to her mouth and squealed. "Oh my goodness. Congratulations! You guys are just about the cutest couple I've ever seen. Drinks are on the house."

Emily reached up to entwine her fingers through Porters. "What do you say to that, Sugar Plum Cake?"

"Well, my Peanut Butter Cookie, I think that sounds mighty dandy." Porter gave Emily's fingers a little squeeze and she leaned in closer. "I figured after three years of marriage; it was finally time to come clean. Especially with Junior Buttercup on the way."

The waitress squealed again. "I'll be right back with those drinks."

Emily could barely breathe by the time the waitress was gone around the corner. She busted out laughing, freeing her hand from Porter's grasp and sitting up straight. "I'm sorry," she said. "It was too hard to resist."

Porter moved his arm off her shoulder and smoothed down the front of his shirt. "I guess I deserve it for the belt buckle joke."

"I feel kind of bad about the free drinks though." It was one thing to tease Porter. It was a different thing entirely to lie to the staff.

"We'll leave a big tip." Porter opened his menu and spread it on the table in front of them. "May as well share a menu since we're officially married now."

Emily liked the way that sounded. One day she planned to get married to someone who made her feel giddy the way Porter did. She knew better than to jump too quickly with the handsome man sitting by her side though. She was still dealing with the aftermath of her messy break up with Gabe. Porter would have to stand the test of time if he was going to be in her future.

"What's your favorite thing on the menu?" Emily couldn't believe how many options there were.

"I'll be honest." Porter leaned in close and lowered his voice. "The food here is kind of average. It's like eating at a cafeteria. It'll fill you up but none of it will be amazing."

That was a first. Most guys pulled out all the stops for their dates, but clearly Porter wasn't bothered.

"So, why did you want to come here?" Emily asked. Maybe it was another prank his brothers had dared him to do.

A waitress walked past carrying a tray of desserts. Clear glass dishes were filled with layer upon layer of cookies, strawberries, and enough ice cream to make a stomach hurt. Fudge and caramel dripped down the sides, with whipped cream piled high on the top.

Porter pointed to the tray. "See that ice cream?"

Emily nodded, her mouth watering as she watched the waitress hand the desserts to a nearby table. It was a wonder the top scoops didn't fall off.

"That is why we are here. The food is average but the desserts are out of this world."

She couldn't wait to dig a spoon into one of the ice cream concoctions. "I guess I'll settle for an average cheeseburger and some fries."

Porter bumped his shoulder against hers. "Are you sure that's what Junior Buttercup wants to eat?"

"I'm sure. What about you, Sugar Plum Cake?" She nudged his shoulder back.

Porter's answer was drowned out by a loud squeal. Their waitress rushed forward, handing over two tall cups of soda.

"You guys are seriously so stinking cute." She dropped a stack of napkins on the table. "I can tell you were meant to be."

Emily glanced at the waitress's name tag. "Thanks,

Lynne. You are too sweet."

"So, did I give you two love birds enough time to read the menu?"

Porter looked at Emily. "I'm ready. How about you, Peanut Butter Cookie? I know you love your cheeseburgers and fries."

That was something he had learned moments before, but Emily went with it. They placed their orders and handed the menu to Lynne. "We're going to need a dessert menu in a while," Porter said.

"You've got it." Lynne rushed away and a companionable silence filled the air.

Emily rested her elbows on the table and looked at Porter. "Do you ever think about it?"

"About what? The food? Not really."

"No. Do you ever think about being married? I thought that was where things were headed with Gabe. Now I'm so relieved it didn't work out."

Porter lifted his cup to his mouth, taking a long time to answer. When he lowered his cup, his eyes had lost their teasing sparkle.

"I *was* married before."

His words shot through Emily. She studied his face, looking for the signs that he was teasing. There was a sadness in his eyes that she didn't think he'd fake. Emily clasped her hands in front of her lap, not sure what to say. Playing pretend married was one thing. The thought of an ex-wife coming across their path was something else entirely. "What happened?"

Porter ran a hand through his hair before he leaned

back in his chair. He rested his hands on the table. "She died."

The words hung in the air, ready for someone to say something, but Emily was finding it difficult to form a coherent thought. She crossed her arms across her stomach, feeling like the air had been punched out of her lungs. This was not what she expected to hear from the man beside her.

CHAPTER 14

The playful mood from moments earlier was gone. Emily rubbed her arm. How could she have been so insensitive? "I can't believe I made up some stupid joke about us being married."

"Why? You didn't know about my past."

He had a point but it didn't help Emily to feel any better. "Yeah, but I shouldn't have been teasing about it. That wasn't okay." If Porter walked out on the date, she'd understand completely.

He reached for her hand, wrapping it between his warm fingers. "It was a harmless mistake. Besides, I don't usually tell people about her until I know someone well. It tends to kill the mood pretty fast."

"I get that. I still feel awful though."

Porter was rubbing circles on her hand with his thumb. "It happened eight years ago. Do you want to hear the story?"

Emily said a silent prayer that she could be supportive

and understanding. Then she nodded. "I want to know everything about you. Even the sad parts."

He cleared his throat. "I dated Cassidy off and on through high school and college. I proposed to her the day I earned my bachelors degree and we were married shortly afterwards. When she was pregnant with our first child, she went into preterm labor. There were complications, and I lost both of them the same day."

"That sounds awful." Emily couldn't imagine the depth of devastation he must have felt. She had buried a grandma but that was the closest she had gotten to death. It had been heartbreaking but her grandma had lived a full life. She wasn't someone with their whole life in front of them.

Porter's thumb hadn't stopped rubbing circles on her hand. He draped his free arm across her shoulders, pulling her close. "This is why I usually don't tell people about Cassidy. It makes people sad."

Emily looked up in shock. "Of course, I'm sad. I don't know how you can be sitting here so calmly. Doesn't it tear you apart?"

Porter let go of her hand and reached for his drink, keeping his arm around her shoulders. He took a sip and then set the cup down, picking up a fork to fiddle with instead.

"You just heard about Cassidy. It is fresh on your mind. For me, it's been eight years. I'm not saying it wasn't hard. The first few years I didn't handle my grief well. I could barely get out of bed. I didn't think I'd be interested in dating ever again. But eventually, my heart began to heal. I still miss Cassidy, but I know she wouldn't want me to spend the rest of my life grieving."

"I still feel like a jerk for making that joke."

Porter rubbed his forehead. "Look. I know we've only known each other for a short time, but I promise you didn't do anything wrong. It makes me happy to be with someone who can joke around with me. You treat me like a regular person and not like someone who is broken."

The way things stood, Emily could choose to believe him or she could shut him down. The thought of not seeing Porter made her realize just how much she really enjoyed being with him. She decided to believe him.

"So, you think you're ready to date someone like me? Even when I say the wrong thing?"

Porter tucked a strand of hair behind her ear, the movement sending a ripple of electricity shooting through her body. He held her gaze, his intensity making it impossible for her to look away.

"Emily, I really like spending time with you. Besides, I'm pretty sure I kicked this whole teasing bit off with that special belt buckle."

Emily leaned her cheek against his hand, letting herself relax. "I can't believe you guys have kept that thing over the years."

"Hey, it's tradition now." Porter's low chuckle sent a wave of longing through Emily. He moved his hand to the back of her head and began to run his fingers through her hair. "We use it as a screening process. If the date can't handle being seen in public with someone looking ridiculous, we figure she probably won't be able to handle the chaos of my family."

"You mean you've worn that thing on more than one date?" Emily could picture the faces of those poor women.

"Hey. It wasn't my idea. Reid started the tradition when my mom was in one of her matchmaking phases. Young ladies kept showing up on the doorstep due to my mom's meddling. He wore the buckle to open the door once, and the poor girl couldn't get away fast enough."

The conversation was interrupted by the arrival of their food. Emily dipped a fry in ranch dressing, eager to see how accurate Porter's assessment of the food was. There was no way it could be as bad as cafeteria food, but as she swallowed her bite, she had to admit he was right. The fries were average at best. She picked up the burger, closing her eyes to really taste the flavors. When she opened them, Porter was watching her.

"So, what do you think?"

Emily looked around to make sure Lynne was nowhere nearby. Then she leaned in close. "Okay. You were right. I'd give the fries a solid seven out of ten. The burger? Maybe a six."

Porter bowed his head towards the surrounding tables. "Thank you, thank you, folks. The next review will come with the ice cream course."

After a few more bites, Emily wiped her mouth with a napkin. "Can I ask you one more thing?"

Porter nodded. "Absolutely. What do you want to know?"

"Did you ever wear the belt for Cassidy? If so, what did she think?"

Porter raised an eyebrow. "We were already dating at the time so she was at the fair with me when Reid won the belt."

"So, she never had to pass the test?"

Porter's eyes lit up. "Let's just say she wasn't the biggest fan when I picked her up for prom in a suit and the belt."

Emily smiled at Porter's stories, but inside her mind was racing. Cassidy wasn't just a wife he had lost. She was his highschool sweetheart. There was no way Emily would be able to compete with that, no matter how many dates she went on with Porter.

The conversation turned to lighter topics, but by the time Lynne brought out their ice cream, Emily's stomach felt sick. The longer she spent with Porter, the more she wanted to be around him. And the more she wanted to be around him, the stronger the little voice in the back of her head shouted that his heart would always belong to someone else.

When Porter walked Emily to the doorstep at the end of the date, her heart was ready to explode. Porter ran a hand through his hair. "Thanks for a fun night."

Emily leaned against the door, taking a final look at the handsome cowboy standing in front of her.

"You were right about that place. The ice cream was worth the mediocre dinner."

"I thought you'd like it." He pulled his keys out of his pocket, turning them over in his hands. "Can I take you out again sometime? I promise to leave the belt buckle behind."

Emily looked into Porter's gorgeous hazel eyes, with flecks of gold highlighted by the early evening sun. "I'd like that a lot," she said. She stepped into Porter's arms, giving him a tight hug. Then she turned and walked into her house, leaving a part of her heart outside with Porter.

* * *

Two days later Emily was at the airport heading to Colorado for her grandpa's birthday party. He was going to be so surprised to see her. She couldn't wait to hug him and tell him how well she and the llamas were settling into their new home.

She hated to admit it, but she also was eager to spend some time away from Porter. Thinking about him made her heart twinge. She couldn't fall for the guy who was still in love with someone else. Despite his assurances, Emily didn't really believe his heart was totally healed. How could it be? Cassidy had been his first true love. They had created a family together. There was no way he could let that go.

The airplane was sitting on the tarmac when she got a message from a very frantic llama sitter. A family emergency had come up and he wasn't going to be able to keep an eye on the ranch. Emily's stomach sank. The aircraft doors closed and she was stuck.

Emily had minutes to find a solution or she'd have to turn around in Colorado and head straight back home. She sent a quick text to Porter explaining the situation. Within seconds of sending the message she got an answer back. Porter assured her that he'd take care of the ranch.

The hum of the engine was getting louder as the plane backed away from the gate. Emily looked up to see a stewardess approaching. "Remember to put your phone in airplane mode until we've landed."

There was no time for Emily to question Porter about his plans. She had no choice but to trust him.

"Yes Ma'am. I'm shutting it off now." Emily said a quick prayer of gratitude that Porter could help and powered down her phone. She plugged in her headphones and leaned against the window, watching the mountains as they got farther and farther away. Somewhere between the fading mountains and the puffy cloud cover that floated beneath the plane, Emily fell asleep.

The plane thudding down woke her up. She deboarded the plane and was in the middle of hugging her mom when her phone chimed with a text message from Porter.

Went to see the llamas. So far they are behaving well. The text was accompanied by a picture of Porter flexing his arms in the foreground while Stephen and Wren grazed in the background.

Emily laughed and showed the picture to her mom.

"You said he has a sense of humor. Somehow, I believe you."

Emily laughed and texted Porter back. **Thanks for checking in. It looks like you are getting along well.**

The next text came through when the family was in the middle of singing happy birthday to her grandpa. She waited until he was cutting slices of cake for everyone before she pulled out her phone to check what Porter had sent.

This time, he was standing in the field next to Bonnie and Cupid. Porter was looking Cupid in the eye, one hand on either side of his face, while Bonnie looked on. **I think I have a new fan.**

There was no reason for a surge of jealousy to shoot through Emily, but she half wished she could swap places with Cupid. She laughed while she typed her reply. **What can I say? He has great tastes.**

Emily tucked her phone into her back pocket, ignoring the raised eyebrows from her sister on the other side of the table. Kayla cornered her on their way to get drink refills.

"What's making you smile? Does it have something to do with your new cowboy friend?"

"Maybe." She pulled out the phone and showed the messages to Kayla.

"He's cuter than I thought," Kayla said.

"You have no idea."

The presents were most of the way opened when Porter texted again. **I'm trying to teach them how to be proper ranch animals. There seems to be a little resistance.** There was a picture attached of Wembley wearing a cowboy hat that looked suspiciously like Porter's.

Emily was holding in her laughter. She didn't want a loud outburst to bring attention to herself. Instead, she held her phone up and turned away from the group so she could take a selfie with her grandpa in the background. She texted it to Porter. **Trying to teach him how to be a proper birthday boy. He seems to be grasping it well.**

She had somehow thought Porter would find a minute or two to check on the animals, but he seemed to have other plans. He certainly didn't need to be spending so much time over there. She wanted to call him but that was going to have to wait until after the party was over.

The guests were filing out for the evening when Emily found a quiet space to sit. She pulled out her phone and sent a quick message to Porter. **Is everything going okay? I feel bad that the llamas are taking you away from your own work.**

She flipped the phone back and forth in her hands, waiting for an answer. There was still no response when her mom came to get her to help with the dishes. It wasn't until she was sitting on the couch next to her grandpa when the next text came through.

Sorry. We were in the middle of story time and the llamas did not want any interruptions. It would have been rude.

Porter sent a picture of himself leaning against the fence, holding up a book. Wren was casually eating the top corner.

Emily was in the middle of a reply when a second picture came through. It was a close up shot of Cupid and Wembley crowding around the book. She could barely make out the title. When she realized it said *Is Your Mama a Llama?* she doubled over laughing.

Her grandpa reached over and rubbed her arm. "What's wrong, sweetheart? Are you okay?"

Emily wiped the tears from her eyes and pulled up the pictures Porter had sent through the day. "I asked my friend to check in on the ranch while I'm here visiting. I think he is having a little too much fun with the llamas."

Her grandpa swiped through the pictures, his smile growing with each one. "Who is this friend of yours?"

Emily could feel the heat rushing to her cheeks. "His name is Porter. I met him recently when a storm blew a tree onto my fence line. His family owns one of the large ranches nearby."

"He looks about your age."

Emily smiled. "Yeah. He's been a good friend to me lately. Do you mind if I answer this text?"

Her grandpa gave her leg a little squeeze. "You take all the time you need."

Emily wrote a quick message. **What was the verdict? Did they decide their mamas were llamas?**

She pushed send and set her phone to the side before plopping her feet on the coffee table in front of her. "Were you surprised by your party, Grandpa?"

"I was. I figured your mom would have a cake for me, but I had no idea how many friends would come. I'm exhausted, but I loved it. You being here was an extra special bonus."

The phone dinged again, and Emily tried to hide her smile.

"Go ahead and check it. You don't want to keep the cowboy waiting."

Emily lifted the phone off the couch. She looked at the picture Porter sent and let out a snort laugh. He was holding the book next to his very sad face, the cover crumpled in one corner. **They agreed they have llama mamas.**

I, on the other hand, will have a very sad mama when I get home with this book. Oops.

Kayla walked in when Emily was typing her response. Emily handed the phone to her sister. "Can you take my picture, please?"

She held her hands in front of her in the shape of a heart, and gave the camera her best pouty face. When Kayla handed the phone back, Emily typed a quick message and hit send along with the picture. **Please tell your mom sorry. The llamas will behave better next time.**

Then she tucked her phone away and turned to see two pairs of eyes watching her.

"It's Porter again, isn't it?" Kayla asked.

Their grandpa nodded. "That's her cowboy's name, right? Porter's a good name. A strong one. I think you'll do okay dating him."

Heat was shooting to the tips of Emily's ears. "Hey, who said anything about dating?"

Kayla snorted. "Well, maybe you should be."

"I agree." Her grandpa pointed to the picture of their grandma hanging on the wall. "Once you find the one, you'll know. Your grandma made me laugh every day of my life."

"Well, it's still way too soon to think about marriage. He does make me laugh though."

Kayla plopped down on the couch and snuggled up against Emily's arm. "If he makes you happy, I approve."

The conversation turned back to the party and how their grandpa was doing. As he talked, Emily let her mind wander. She could see a glimpse of the future with Porter, but she was afraid to trust him with her emotions. He had a lot more to overcome than a silly girlfriend from the past. Was his heart really in shape for a real commitment?

Only time would tell.

CHAPTER 15

The sun was casting deep shadows when Porter finally climbed into his truck. Emily's animals had all been fed and watered. There was a lot of work to finish at his own ranch, but the time he had taken to help Emily was certainly worth it. Her reactions to his text messages seemed to indicate that she was pleased with his efforts.

The truck had been idling for a few minutes but Bree still hadn't come out of the barn. If she didn't show up soon, he was going to get a lecture from Thomas. After a few minutes he honked the horn. There was still no sight of Bree. He had his hand on the door handle when she came tearing around the corner, her dark brown curls bouncing on her shoulders as she slid into the passenger's seat.

"Her llamas are so sweet!" Bree said. She was covered with specks of hay, but her grin was huge. "I can't believe Emily let you take care of them."

"They are pretty cool creatures. Thanks for giving me a hand." Porter was thrilled that Emily had asked him for help. She probably could have left them alone, but the alternative had been much more fun to Porter.

Bree waved her camera in the air. "I got so many good shots for my photography class, everyone is going to be jealous."

Porter pulled his phone out to show her Emily's last response. "I think Emily liked those photos too."

"She gave you heart hands?" Bree clasped her hands to her chest. "That means she really likes you."

"Or it means she's grateful that I'm taking care of her animals."

Bree rolled her eyes. "Whatever. She totally has a crush on you."

The thought of Emily having a crush on him was something he could get used to. "I guess we'll see. Things got pretty serious on our date so I was hoping to make her smile. Thanks to you and your photo skills, I think we accomplished that."

Bree waved her phone towards Porter, making the glitter in her case swirl. "I got awesome pictures for Emily and a few good blackmail pictures for my collection, too." She swiped through the phone, showing a picture to Porter. "Like this one."

Porter was sitting on the ground precariously close to a pile of horse manure. He had climbed over a fence and was walking across the field when his boot got stuck in a gopher hole. One slight tug was all it took to send him tumbling to the ground. He narrowly missed the manure, but the look of disgust on his face was captured perfectly by Bree.

"You're going to delete that, right?"

"Not a chance." Bree swiped through a few more photos, stopping to show Porter another one. "I totally thought Wembley was going to bite your hand when you tried to put that hat on him. Look at how you are pleading with him to cooperate."

Thankfully Porter's sense of humor let him appreciate how silly he looked. "I'm glad you came with me. Thanks for making so many visits today."

"I loved it, but if Thomas and Reid are frustrated with us, I'm blaming you."

"I'll work extra fast this evening to make it up to them."

Porter turned his truck down Old Ranch Road as the sun was setting behind the mountains. The tops of the mountains were still covered in snow, but the spring flowers were in full bloom. He drove past the Landon ranch, slowing down when they came to the stretch of land that was covered in tulips. A number of cars were stopped on the side of the road with people hanging out their windows to take pictures.

Bree had been silent for most of the drive home, which was unusual for the normally talkative girl. Porter glanced over at her.

"What's on your mind?"

She turned to Porter. "How do you know if you're in love with someone?"

"That's a pretty deep thought for the day."

"I know, but I really am curious. I mean, you obviously like Emily. How will you know if you love her?"

It would be easy to make a joke, but Bree's face seemed a little too serious. Porter rubbed his chin. "I don't know, sis. The last woman I was truly in love with was Cassidy."

"Then you know what falling in love feels like."

They drove past the last of the tulips and headed up the hill towards the ranch. Porter's mind was searching for the right answer. "I think falling in love feels different for each person. With Cassidy, I knew her for almost as long as I could remember. I never gave love a thought until one day when we were hanging out. We were sitting on the couch and laughing. At that moment, I realized that I'd rather spend time doing nothing with Cassidy than go on some grand adventure with anyone else. Once I realized that, I was hooked. She could have asked me for the moon and I would have found a way to bring it to her."

Bree sighed. "I don't remember a lot about her. I mean, I had fun when you guys came over but I don't remember a lot of details. I know she was always super nice to me."

"She was something special. As for Emily, I'm trying not to put any pressure on the relationship. I've only seen her a few times. It's way too soon to call it love."

"But at least you can say you like her, right?"

Porter's mouth lifted. "Yeah. I really do." The thought of her getting all of his goofy texts made his heart happy. He almost wished her trip was longer, but then he wouldn't get to spend time with Emily in person. He turned his attention back to Bree. "Why are you asking these questions? Is there a secret boyfriend you're hiding from us?"

Bree nodded her head. "Not just one, but five. I'm trying to figure out which one I love the most." She laughed. "Really, there are a few cute guys at my school, but I'm not ready to date anyone seriously yet. I was just curious."

Porter pulled into his spot on the driveway and turned the engine off. He reached over to squeeze Bree's arm. "I tell you what. If I fall in love with Emily, you'll be the first person in the family I tell."

"Pinky promise?"

Porter wrapped his finger through hers and shook it. "Pinky promise."

The smile on Bree's face made the inconvenience of all the trips to Emily's ranch worth it.

* * *

THE SUN HAD DROPPED behind the mountains when Porter finished the last of his jobs. He was taking off his boots when his phone began to ring. A quick glance at the caller ID had him taking the stairs to his room two steps at a time. "Hi, Emily," he said, pulling his door closed behind him. He sat on the edge of his bed. "How was the party?"

Emily talked in a hushed voice. "It's been a blast. I snuck away for a few minutes to check in. Did the animals give you any trouble?"

"Apart from nibbling on the edge of my book, they were perfect. There were no escape attempts and no fighting that I could see."

Emily's soft laugh sent a wave of longing through him.

He had told Bree he liked Emily, but it was deeper than that. Spending time with her made his day brighter.

"I'm glad they were on their best behavior."

Porter slid across the bed so he was sitting with his back against the headboard. "When do you get home?"

"My flight lands around four in the afternoon. If you add in driving time and traffic, I figure I should be home no later than five. I'll be able to do the evening check in."

"Do you need a ride back from the airport?"

"Nope. I'm good. I left my car in the long-term parking lot."

Porter pushed away the feeling of disappointment of not having a long car ride with Emily to look forward to. He'd get to see her soon enough.

Emily cleared her throat. "I'd better get back to my family. Thanks again for everything, Porter. I really appreciate it."

"Any time." Porter hung up the phone and pulled out a notebook. He had started a list of things to make Emily smile. If Emily wasn't coming home until later in the day, he had time for one more surprise.

* * *

RED PAINT WAS SMEARED down Porter's arm when he stepped back to survey his work. He hoped it was the color Emily had really wanted on the barn. It was risky choosing to paint a building to impress a woman. Reid had told him so in no uncertain terms. So had Thomas. Only Bree had been on his side.

"Guys. She already picked the color and bought the paint. It was sitting there, begging Porter to use it." Bree wiped the back of her hand across her face, adding a streak of red to her forehead.

"You may be right," Thomas said. "But what if it is there because she hated the color and changed her mind. Maybe she didn't paint yet because she didn't like it."

Porter grinned at his siblings. "If she hates it, then I guess I'll be asking you all to pitch in and help repaint the thing."

Thomas groaned. "Is she really worth all the trouble?"

Porter nodded. "I think so. Even if the relationship doesn't go anywhere, we're helping a neighbor. That's always good."

"You've got a point," Reid said. "I, for one, am rooting for you."

"Me too," Bree said.

"I appreciate that. Now, I can handle the clean up here if you guys want to get back to the ranch. Tell Mom I'll probably be late for dinner."

The siblings climbed into their car and drove off. Porter stepped back to snap a photo of their handiwork. It had taken them a little over an hour with everyone helping to paint the first coat on the small barn. He pulled out his phone to check the time. If Emily's flight was on time, there were about fifteen minutes to clean up and leave before she got home.

Porter was setting the second ladder in the back of his truck when Emily pulled up next to him. One look at her flushed face had his stomach doing somersaults.

Emily climbed out of the car. "Hi. I said I'd be home in time for the afternoon check in. I didn't want you to have to take more time out of your day to help."

Her hair was down, the long strands catching the afternoon sun. Porter's breath hitched in his throat. "You did. I'll be out of your way in just a second."

Emily's smile sent a wave of longing through Porter. All Bree's talk of him falling in love was messing with his emotions. He hadn't given himself permission to hope for a real relationship with anyone after the number of bad dates he'd been on, but looking at Emily's face made him rethink the possibilities.

"You're fine being here. I just wasn't expecting to see anyone but I'm glad I get to say hi to you."

Porter held his arms out and Emily stepped into his embrace. He held her close for a moment before letting her go.

"Mind if I tag along while you check on everyone?" Porter wanted to see Emily's reaction when she discovered the barn.

"I'd love it." Emily slipped out of her tennis shoes and pulled on a pair of boots that were sitting outside the office door. "You can tell me how you got my llamas to actually pose with you. They aren't exactly the most cooperative of creatures."

Porter laughed. "Bree was my secret weapon. She's so bossy, even the llamas obeyed her." He followed Emily to the fence. The llamas were hanging out at the far side of the field, but as soon as Emily whistled, they came running.

Wren was the first to arrive. She leaned her face over the fence, letting out a soft trill.

Emily placed a hand on either side of Wren's face. "Were you good for Porter?" she asked, rubbing behind Wren's tan ears.

"She was perfect," Porter said.

Bonnie and Stephen trotted up beside Wren and immediately tried to push her out of the way so they could be near Emily. Emily chided the llamas. "Wait your turn. There's plenty of cuddles to go around." Even as she spoke, she was reaching out to greet them.

Watching Emily with her llamas was incredibly endearing. Porter had dated a few too many women who shrieked if they got so much as a speck of dust on their manicured hands. Emily didn't seem to care that her llamas had been rolling on the ground and were covered with pieces of dried brush. Her love for the llamas was evident.

He pulled out his phone and snapped a quick picture of Emily with her cheek pressed close to Stephen's face. Her hair hung down in curtains, hiding most of her face, but their special bond was evident.

Emily straightened up as Porter was tucking his phone back into his pocket. "Want to go look for the rest of them?" he asked. The farthest fields passed right by the newly painted barn.

"Let's go."

Porter followed Emily along the fence line. They were getting close to the barn when Emily stopped, putting a hand over her mouth. She turned to Porter; her eyes wide. "What did you do?"

Porter's stomach began to roll. He hoped she'd like it. "I saw the paint bucket and had a little extra time on my hands. I should have asked first."

Emily planted her hands on her hips, her brow furrowed. "Yes, you should have." She frowned at Porter and his stomach filled with lead.

"We can repaint it," Porter said. He took his hat off and held it against his chest, knowing his hair was probably sticking up all over the place. He could barely meet Emily's eye.

She took a step forward. "I could have done the job myself."

"I know." Porter debated about hightailing it out of there but he stood his ground. He'd take his reprimand like a man.

She stepped forward again. "I am perfectly capable of taking care of this ranch on my own."

"I know," Porter said again. He put his hat back on so he could hold up both hands. "Emily, you are one of the most capable women I've ever met. I wasn't implying anything about your work ethic."

Emily took another step so she was inches from his face. "What is it with you cowboys and your need to fix everything?"

Her face was turned towards Porter's, with her lips tantalizingly close to his own. He gulped. "Honestly, I don't know. I can't help it if it's for someone I like." The words were out but Porter didn't want to take them back.

Emily bit her lip, a frown on her face. Then she stepped back. "You like me?"

Porter held back a smile. "Maybe a little."

"Huh." She stared him down but Porter held his ground. It was difficult to concentrate on her disappointment while she was standing so close to him. One slight move and his arms would be wrapped around her waist.

A moment later Emily smiled. "I can't believe you'd do this for me. I was dreading that job."

Porter's stomach began to unclench. "You didn't want to paint the barn?"

"Oh, I wanted it painted. I just didn't want to be the one on the ladder. I like my feet planted firmly on the ground."

He folded his arms across his chest. "Emily Hutchings, you are the most complicated woman I've met. I'm not sure if I want to toss you over that fence or kiss that sassy mouth of yours."

He knew which one he'd choose.

"Those are my only two options?" She stepped forward and his arms ached to pull her close.

Porter was finding it difficult to make words. "Yep."

Emily tilted her lips up so they were an inch from Porter's. His pulse raced. She placed her hands on his chest and slid them up to his shoulders, leaving a trail of heat where she touched.

"And you can't think of any other options for me?"

Porter shook his head, finding it difficult to concentrate on anything other than her lips. "I'm afraid not."

Emily pushed away from Porter with a laugh and began to run. "Then I guess you're going to have to throw me over that fence. But first, you'll have to catch me."

CHAPTER 16

Emily's heart was about to explode. She was running away from Porter, but all she could think about was the moment when he'd catch her. Their chemistry was undeniable. She had been falling for him since the moment she saw him, but the llama pictures were what put her over the edge. The guy was playful, charming, and irresistible.

It took all of her will power to have her face so close to Porter's and not kiss him. She'd been wondering about how his lips would feel when she finally caved in. Sure, he had a complicated past, but the way he was looking at her didn't leave much room for doubt.

She was running around the corner of the barn when Porter finally caught up to her. He pinned her against the wall, his chest heaving. Then he bent down and scooped her up into his strong arms, turning to take long strides towards the fence.

Emily let out an involuntary shriek. "I changed my

mind," she said. Her stomach was dancing with nerves but she knew what she wanted.

Porter stopped walking. He held her in his arms and jerked his head towards the fence. "Are you sure? We're almost there."

She reached her hand out and rested it on Porter's chest, feeling his heart racing beneath his shirt. "Yeah. I'm sure."

Porter grunted, and then he turned back to the barn. He set Emily down, his eyes never leaving hers.

Emily reached for Porter's hat, taking it off his head so she could tangle her fingers in his hair. He wrapped his arms around her, pressing her back so she was trapped between the warm wood of the barn and his strong body.

The tension was tangible, but Porter still didn't kiss her. He brought his hand forward and tucked her hair behind her ear. Then he slid his hand along her cheek, his calloused hand gentle with his touch.

Emily closed her eyes and leaned into his hand. She pressed her cheek against his skin, aching for the kiss that was inevitable. If she had to wait much longer, she was going to implode into a million little pieces.

Porter's voice was low when he finally spoke. "If you insist."

She took a breath and Porter's lips met hers. The kiss was filled with a hunger that came from two people long deprived of affection. His lips weren't gentle but neither were hers. Emily wrapped her hands in his hair, pulling him closer, and Porter responded. He pressed his hand against her waist and closed the space between them until all she could feel was the heat of his body wrapped against hers.

Emily shoved down her disappointment when Porter pulled back. He let go of Emily's waist and turned to lean against the barn wall beside her, his breathing ragged.

"So. That happened," he said.

Emily's face was flooded with heat, from the barn to Porter's warm body to the way he made her feel. She held her hand to her cheeks. "I didn't mind."

"Me either. I guess that was more fun than tossing you over the fence."

"You guess?" Emily spun around to face Porter.

He leaned down to grab his cowboy hat off the ground and dusted it off. "I mean, I don't have anything to compare it to."

He raised his eyebrow and Emily smacked his arm. "Don't get any crazy ideas. This was a one time choice."

"Does that mean the kissing bit was a one-time choice as well?" Porter's face was irresistible.

Emily stood on her tiptoes and gave him a soft kiss on the cheek. "I sure hope not. I think we could make an exception for a little more of that."

"I agree." Porter reached for her hand, placing a kiss on each of her fingers before spinning her to face him. He lowered his chin, and Emily forgot everything except for the way his lips moved against hers.

*　*　*

HER LIPS WERE STILL TINGLING when Emily woke up the next morning. She could definitely add kissing the cowboy to her list of things she enjoyed a lot. She stretched out in bed, going through her jobs for the day. With the Llama Center for Healing opening in six weeks, Emily had a lot to work on to get ready. If she didn't moderate her time with Porter, she could easily get lost in his gold-flecked eyes and forget her responsibilities.

Emily poured water into her coffee maker and pushed the button. She pulled out her laptop to browse bright pink halters for the llamas while she waited. The center owned a few of the standard black halters, but sometimes patients wanted something more cheerful. It was a simple purchase that was sure to make at least a few people smile.

When the timer dinged, Emily poured her coffee into a portable mug and headed to the llama center. She was pulling up to the house when she noticed a small glass vase sitting on her porch with a single pink and white tulip inside. A handwritten note leaned up against the side.

It would be my pleasure if you would accompany me on a walk this afternoon. I have something special I'd like to show you. - Porter

Emily lifted the tulip to her nose and inhaled, surprised by how powerful the small flower smelled. The tulips she planted in her yard were usually odorless. She unlocked the door and brought the vase inside, setting it on a table in what was now the waiting room. The day was barely beginning and Porter was already making her smile.

Her mood didn't waver when she discovered that she had left the water on overnight, flooding the last flower bed she had planted. She prayed the plants would survive so she didn't have to plant another bed.

The good mood started to wane when she found Stephen rolling in a patch of brambles; his fur covered with sharp barbs. Brushing him was one more thing to add to the steadily growing list of things to do. As she brushed out his fur, she daydreamed about what Porter had planned.

By the time the afternoon came, Emily's arms were sore from lugging around supplies. She was trying to fix one of the stall doors when Porter arrived. He stepped up behind her, wrapping her in a hug, and Emily leaned into him, her tension melting away.

"Is it strange to say I missed you?" she asked. She bit the side of her cheek, feeling suddenly self-conscious of her sweaty shirt and messy ponytail.

"Not if I say it back." Porter kissed the top of her head. "I've been waiting all day until I could come see you."

"I'm glad you are here." Emily wrapped her arms around his waist. "I believe I was promised some sort of a walk?"

"You were. Do you need help finishing up here?"

Emily shook her head. "I have four more bolts to tighten and then I'll be ready. You can stand to the side and look pretty."

"Got it." He walked to the other end of the stall and struck a pose, one hand on his hip and the other behind his head. "How's this?"

Emily's laughter bubbled to the surface. "Perfection." She tightened the first bolt, trying to keep a straight face.

How was she so lucky to have Porter standing in her barn? She moved to the second bolt and Porter changed poses.

"And now?" He was facing backwards, his hip jutted to the side while he looked over his shoulder. One hand covered his mouth.

Emily snort-laughed. "Are you sure you want to be a cowboy? I think there is a modeling career in there for you somewhere." She moved to the third bolt, watching out of the corner of her eye to see what Porter did next.

He lifted one leg and rested it on a bale of straw, folding both arms in front of his chest while he scowled off into the distance.

Emily fanned her face. "How am I supposed to work with such raw talent in front of me?" She moved to the fourth bolt, her stomach bubbling with laughter.

"Final one?" he asked.

Emily nodded. "Yep. Final one."

Porter slid to the floor and lay on his stomach, propping his elbows up so he could cup both hands together under his chin. He kicked his legs up behind him, slowly moving them back and forth in the air.

That was the final crack to Emily's composure. She tightened the bolt and threw the wrench to the side so she could applaud Porter's efforts. He hopped up and bowed to the audience of one.

Emily went to Porter and helped brush bits of straw off the front of his shirt. He definitely deserved a reward for that show. She stood on her tiptoes and gave him a kiss on the cheek, feeling suddenly self-conscious.

"I think I'm ready for that walk now." Emily said. "Are you?"

Porter nodded. He held his hand out. When Emily laced her fingers through his, her heart sped up. Walking hand in hand with the cowboy felt almost more intimate than their kiss the day before.

"My truck is this way."

Emily stopped and looked at Porter with a furrowed brow. "I believe I was promised a walk. Not a drive."

"Don't worry." Porter squeezed Emily's fingers. "There will be plenty of walking once we get there."

Emily gave him a reassuring smile. It didn't matter where they were going as long as she got to go with Porter.

She climbed into the truck and put the seatbelt on, ready for an adventure. Five minutes later they were pulling onto Old Ranch Road. Once Emily realized where they were headed, her stomach began to churn. She was excited about her budding relationship with Porter, but it was way too early to meet his family.

"Uh, Port? I know I said hi to your mom once but I'm not exactly dressed for a real conversation." The grass stains on her jeans were an extra special look that she didn't usually pull out when trying to make a good impression.

Porter gave her hand a reassuring squeeze. "I know better than to spring the whole family on someone without warning." He pulled to the side of the road, parking behind a red sedan. "We're here."

Emily's curiosity grew when she began counting cars alongside the road. "What on earth?" she asked.

Porter reached for her hand and Emily let herself be pulled forward. They were getting close to the front of the first car when Emily saw them. Rows of tulips lined the road, stretching as far as the eye could see.

The sight was breathtaking. "They are beautiful. Why are they here?"

Porter pulled her around a couple that had stopped at the front of the tulip rows to take a picture. "What do you know about the families that live on this road?"

Emily was brought back to the conversation she'd overheard in the store weeks ago. "Not much. I have heard that the three largest ranching families live up here. And I know you belong to one of those families." Heat rose in her cheeks. It sounded like she had been doing her research to check him out.

"You're right. Back in the early 1900's my ancestor Gabriel Matthews claimed over 20,000 acres of land with his best friends Michael Landon and Jeremy Stringham. Together they owned the largest cattle ranching operation in the state."

Emily tried to picture that many acres but she had no frame of reference. "How much land is that?"

"It's pretty much double the size of our town."

That was more land than Emily could ever dream of owning. "So, your relative owned a city or two. It's three ranches now. When did the land split?"

"The oldest daughter on the Matthews side married one

of the Stringham sons. Their dads split off part of the land as a wedding present."

"Wow. That's pretty cool. So, you're related to everyone up here?"

Porter gave her hand a squeeze. "Not quite, but I consider them all family."

They walked past a windmill nestled amidst the tulips. Emily stopped to admire the way the sails spun around in a circle, moving to an almost imperceptible breeze. She kept hold of Porter's hand while they walked, ignoring the looks that people shot their way.

When they reached a break in the tulips, Porter tilted his head towards hers. "Do you want to go the secret way?" His voice was a low whisper.

Emily shivered with delight. "Obviously. Secrets are the best."

He walked to a large flowering bush and then gently pushed a handful of branches to the side. A small gate was hidden behind the bush. Porter pushed it open and waved his hand. "After you," he said.

Emily walked through the gate and turned to wait for Porter. He carefully closed the latch behind them. When he turned back to face Emily, he wore a guilty expression like a kid who had been caught doing something naughty.

"Are you sure this is okay?" Emily asked. "Are we trespassing on some old farmer's land and we're going to come face to face with a shotgun?"

"I wouldn't put you in any real danger." Porter rested his hand on her waist.

"Is this your property and we're secretly meeting your family?"

"Not quite. You asked if I was related to everyone up here. We're on the Landon ranch right now. Back in the thirties the family adopted a son. He inherited this property and married a woman from Holland."

The pieces were clicking into place. It made sense that she'd bring the spirit of her home to Utah. "So, do you usually trespass on the Landon's property?"

"It isn't trespassing if you helped plant the tulips." Porter winked at her. "They have a separate field that you can't see from the road."

Emily's heart began to race. The flowers along the road had been pretty enough. She couldn't imagine how beautiful an entire field would be.

CHAPTER 17

Porter liked the way Emily fit next to him. He wrapped his arm around her shoulders and turned towards the path that led to the tulip field. The flowers along the road were a gift to the city, but the tulips behind the gate were for close friends and family only. If Porter had his timing right, they'd be able to walk through the fields without any other people around.

He guided Emily along the trail that had been worn down from years of use. Porter stopped Emily when they were almost to the flowers. "Do you trust me?"

She laughed. "It depends on what I'm trusting you to do. Do I trust you to give Stephen a proper hair cut? Probably not."

Porter cupped a hand under her chin, tilting her face towards his. "Do you trust me to guide you along the rest of this path with your eyes closed? I want to show you the tulips from the best spot, and that involves keeping your eyes closed until we are there."

He held her face, wanting to plant a kiss on the lips that were turning down into a frown but he held back.

"What if I trip?" Emily's brow wrinkled with concern. "I can't get hurt right before the llama center opens."

Porter flexed his arm, laughing as he did so. "I'd say I'm strong enough to keep you from falling."

Emily placed a hand on his arm to squeeze his muscles, which sent small tingles racing through his veins.

"Fine. I'll trust you but I better not get hurt."

There was a challenge behind her tone that Porter didn't understand. He lifted Emily's chin so he could see her eyes. "What's wrong?"

She looked away, biting the side of her cheek. "It's nothing."

"It's clearly something." He wished he could understand what was holding Emily back. "It's okay if you'd rather walk beside me with your eyes open."

Emily cleared her throat. "This is going to sound stupid, but the last guy who asked me to trust him ended up hurting me pretty badly." Emily looked away from Porter.

"You mean Gabe?" Porter slid his hand from Emily's chin to her shoulder and began to massage it gently.

"Yeah." Emily tilted her cheek down so it rested against Porter's hand. "I know you guys are two totally different people, but it is hard to let go of those fears."

Her words resonated with him. "I understand. Probably more than you think. I don't have an ex who treated me poorly, but I do have a lot of scars from people letting me down."

"So where does that leave us?" Emily lifted her head to look at him.

"I think it means we start small. How about this? I promise I will get you to the tulip fields without you getting hurt."

She took a deep breath. "Okay. I promise to let you guide me. I won't even peek."

Porter held out his hand with his pinky extended. "Pinky promise?" he asked.

Emily held her finger out. "Pinky promise." She grinned when he shook it up and down. "Are we seven?"

"I blame Bree. She's been having us make pinky promises since she was a little girl. I'll have you know; this is a binding agreement."

There was an intensity when Emily answered. "I take my promises seriously."

Her words thudded against his heart, reminding him of the gravity of the situation. He had promised safety and he'd deliver, even if it meant throwing her over his shoulder and carrying her all the way. He pulled Emily close and kissed the top of her head. "Ready?"

"I'm ready."

As Emily closed her eyes, Porter's heart surged. The trust she was putting in him felt much larger than a simple promise to guide her along the path. He placed her hand on the crook of his elbow and pulled her forward.

The path narrowed the closer they got to the field. Porter helped Emily sidestep a rock that was in the way. They were moving along at a steady pace until they reached a fallen log. Porter looked at the log and then down at Emily. He slowed her to a stop and released her arm.

"Are you doing okay?"

Emily turned her face towards his voice, her eyes still closed. "So far, so good."

"Alright. I'm going to talk you through this next part."

Porter reached both his hands out, taking Emily's hands in his. "There's a log here in our way. I'm going to place your hands on the top of it and then help you slide over."

Emily squeezed his hands tightly, not letting go. "I'm not going to squish any caterpillars or other gross creatures, am I?"

He rubbed his thumbs on her hands, trying to hold back a laugh. "It's just rough bark from the side of the tree."

"Okay. But if I touch anything slimy, I'm out of here."

Porter guided Emily over the final obstacle and his heart soared. He helped her place her hands and then guided her hips over the log. The tulips were dancing in the field to his left but Porter wanted Emily to experience the full panoramic view. He placed her hand on his arm and pulled her forward.

"One more minute and we are there."

When they reached the point of the path that gave the best view, Porter slowed Emily to a stop. "We made it." He lifted Emily's hand off his arm and wrapped his fingers through hers.

"Can I open my eyes now?"

Porter looked down at her face, ready to catch her expression. "You can open them."

Emily opened her eyes slowly, as if she was afraid of what she would see. Then her mouth dropped open.

Porter could feel her awe while she turned her face from side to side.

After a moment of stunned silence, Emily spoke. "Porter, this is gorgeous."

He grinned. "I agree. My family has been helping plant tulips with the Landons for years."

"How many tulips are there?"

"We don't really know. When she was little my sister Hope decided to count all the flowers. By the time she made it to 300, she got overwhelmed and stopped. Best guess, there are well over 15,000 bulbs."

The expression on Emily's face warmed Porter's heart completely. When his truck had gone sliding off the road, he hadn't been able to see God's hand in it. Now, standing with Emily, he could understand how the Lord had been steering them towards each other all along. Every interaction with her reminded him what it felt like to be with someone he wanted to protect.

"Do you want to see my favorite spot?"

Emily nodded. "I can't wait."

Porter pointed to a barely perceptible path that wove through the tulips. They walked up a small hill and stopped at the top to see the flowers that cascaded down the back side of the hill.

Emily took in a sharp breath. "I don't think I've ever seen anything more beautiful in my life."

"I agree." Porter was studying Emily's face, but he

quickly turned to the flowers. She would think he was way too cheesy if she caught him staring.

They followed the path to a small gazebo that was nestled off to one side. Porter held Emily's hand as she walked up a couple of steps to the center platform. From their vantage point, tulips stretched to both sides, with fiery red, vibrant yellow, and deep purple flowers fading into the distance. The most fragrant tulips had been planted next to the gazebo, filling the air with an intoxicating aroma.

He stepped behind Emily, wrapping his arms around her waist while she leaned against his back. As they swayed back and forth, looking at the nature surrounding them, Porter could feel the final pieces of his heart mending together. He hadn't believed he would ever love again after Cassidy. For years, he hadn't even been interested. Now, feeling the way Emily fit against him, Porter felt hope for the future.

Emily turned to face him and clasped her hands behind his neck. "This truly is a gift. Thank you."

When she tilted her chin up, Porter wasted no time responding. He kissed her gently and then held her close, letting the sun press against his back while he enjoyed the moment with the woman he was falling for.

* * *

PORTER WAS HOLDING Emily's hand when they emerged from the secret gate a couple of hours later. The sun was starting to cast long shadows across the mountains, and a breeze had picked up. They had walked along every path they could find, easily getting lost in the sea of flowers.

He was latching the gate behind them when he heard a familiar voice coming from the other side of the bushes. Why was Thomas hanging around the tulip fields?

A sinking feeling slowed his steps. Emily had specifically said she wasn't ready to meet the family, and yet, judging from the sound of the other voices that joined Thomas's, half his family was on the other side of the hedge.

Emily was walking forward but Porter reached for her arm, gently pulling her back. "So, remember how I said we weren't going to meet my family today?"

She nodded. "Yeah."

Porter didn't think his stomach could sink any further, but apparently it could. "Well, I think my family decided to come here."

The laughing voices were getting louder.

Emily looked over her shoulder and then back at Porter, confusion written on her face. "I don't see anyone."

"But you can hear them. They are on the other side of the hedge." Porter's mind was searching through all his options. If he knew his family at all, they were heading right for the secret gate. He had maybe a minute until they ducked around the side of the bushes and found Porter standing close to an extremely confused Emily.

He could slip back through the gate with Emily, but there really wasn't anywhere to hide on the other side of the fence. Porter wished he could part the hedge and step through, but the foliage was too dense. They would get leaves in their hair and sticks stabbing their backs while their backsides hung out in the open.

Emily stepped closer to Porter, turning to look over her shoulder again.

They had maybe thirty seconds left. Porter placed a quick kiss on Emily's forehead, fervently praying that it wouldn't be the last time he was able to do that. She had every right to be mad at him for what he was about to do.

"I am so, so sorry," he said. He pulled her from their hiding spot between the hedge and fence, coming face to face with his family.

A voice cleared on the other side of the fence as Mr. Landon also approached. Porter silently cursed his timing. Five minutes earlier and they would have left undetected.

"Hi, Emily," Mom said. She stepped past her children and wrapped Emily in a hug. "It's so good to see you again."

Mr. Landon rested his elbows on the fence. "And who is this lovely young lady?"

Porter scanned the ground, waiting for a hole to magically open up and swallow them. Between the red flush filling Emily's cheeks and her tight grip on his hand, he knew she'd welcome a gaping pit over the torture they were experiencing at the moment.

Emily shot him a look of pure panic and Porter's brain kicked in. "Guys, this is my friend Emily. Emily, meet my neighbor Mr. Landon. I think you know some of my crew. This is my mom, Thomas, Reid, and Bree."

He pulled Emily back a step from the family while the men tipped their hats towards her. "I was just showing her the tulip fields," he said.

Another voice called out. "Who were you showing my fields?" Mrs. Landon appeared from behind the bushes.

"Mrs. Landon, this is my friend Emily." Porter glanced over his shoulder, waiting for the pastor or the local grocer to appear. Everyone else seemed to be coming by.

Emily squeezed Porter's hand tighter, but she didn't let go. "The tulips are incredible," Emily said. "Thank you for letting us see them."

"That's where we're headed right now," Bree said. "Want to come?"

Porter didn't have to look at Emily's face to know the answer. "We were actually headed home. Emily has some things she needs to take care of on her ranch and I've got a few more jobs to finish up back home."

Mom stepped forward, including both of them in her hug this time. "It was so good to see you, Emily. I hope you'll come by the ranch some time."

Emily nodded. "I'd like that."

Porter stood with Emily, not saying a word while they waited for his family to slip behind the bushes. Then he wrapped his arm around her waist, breathing in the comforting scent of her floral shampoo. When the chattering of the voices faded to a quiet whisper, Porter turned Emily to face him.

He tucked a strand of hair behind her ear, letting his hand linger on the back of her neck. "How much trouble am I in?" he asked.

Emily cocked her head to the side, studying Porter with a look that left his insides churning. "A bit," she said. "But I think I know a way you can make it up to me."

Emily ran a hand down Porter's arm and he responded the best way he knew. He grabbed her hand and wrapped it around his waist. Then he leaned down and kissed her face slowly, starting at the top of her head and working his way down to her jaw line.

"Is this close?" he asked. He pressed a kiss under her chin, enjoying the way her breath hitched in her throat.

"Mmm. I'm not sure." Emily's hand traveled up his back, leaving a trail of heat where she touched.

He kissed the side of her neck, nuzzling his face into her hair. Then he gently moved to whisper in her ear. "How about now?"

A quivering sigh left Emily's lips and Porter was undone. He kissed the side of her cheek and then found her lips, showing her just how sorry he was that they had been in such an awkward situation.

It wasn't until a car drove by, with people honking the horn and cheering, that Porter remembered where they were standing. There were people nearby who had come to admire the flowers. Thanks to Porter and Emily, they had also gotten a show.

Porter gave Emily a final, gentle kiss and then pulled back, clearing his throat. "I should probably take you home before we get the entire town talking." He knew he should feel some sort of chagrin that they had been caught making out on the side of the road, but all Porter felt was elation. He couldn't wait to drive Emily home so he could continue his apology.

CHAPTER 18

The clouds were moving slowly across the sky. Emily was envious of their lazy pace. She glanced at her phone and growled. The past hour had flown by and she wasn't much closer to finishing her list for the day. Every time she'd get through one task, three more would pop up to fill the space. Even though the list kept growing, there was one item she was accomplishing every day, rain or shine.

Spending time with Porter had made the top of the list. It didn't matter if it was a quick kiss to say hello or a more elaborate date. All she knew was that if she fit seeing Porter somewhere into her day, the day would go much better. He was due to arrive any minute and Emily couldn't wait.

Two weeks had passed since the tulip fields, and Porter was still apologizing. Between lazy walks around the ranch and dates at various places in the town, Emily had been learning a lot about Porter. One thing was for certain. He really didn't like to let people down. She didn't know how to help him believe that it wasn't his fault his family had shown up to visit the tulips.

He was kissing her against the side of the barn when she held her hand up. "Enough is enough."

Porter flinched. "No more kissing?"

The thought made her stomach clench. "No more apologizing. It was awkward having your family catch me off guard, but I was over it an hour later."

He tilted his head to the side and rubbed his chin. "What I'm hearing is that I need a new reason to be kissing you."

Emily laughed and ran her hands through his hair. She loved the feel of his soft, curly waves of hair in contrast to his stubbly 5 o'clock shadow. "Do we need a reason?"

Porter stepped back, keeping his arm around her shoulder. "I don't know. I may need to apologize again after I ask you something."

His face was so serious, Emily's heart dropped. "What's wrong?"

He shifted his weight to his other foot. "At the risk of sounding too pushy, my mom has been begging me to have you over ever since they caught us by the tulips. Would you like to come to my house for dinner this week?"

A knee jerk reaction of panic shot through her body. She took a few seconds to calm her breathing before she could answer. "Are you sure they want to meet me?"

Porter nodded. "They want to know who I'm spending all my spare time with."

"Okay. I can do that." If meeting the family made Porter

happy, she'd be there. "I guess this time I'll have warning so I look presentable when I go over. Your mom might not recognize me without paint in my hair or stains on my jeans."

Porter pushed her hair behind her ear and she held back a soft shiver. Somehow, he managed to warm up nerve endings along the side of her scalp that she didn't know existed.

His voice was low when he leaned down to whisper in her ear. "You always look beautiful to me."

Emily let the compliment wash over her. It felt good having someone around who cared. "Thanks, but I'd like to look nice to someone other than you. What day works best?"

Porter's hesitation was endearing. "Is tonight too soon?" he asked.

A surge of adrenaline shot through Emily's body. "Doesn't your mom need some warning?"

Porter shook his head. "Nah. It's my mom. She's always cooking enough to feed a small army. Leftovers rarely last more than a day or two between me and my brothers."

Emily turned her back to Porter, leaning against his chest while his arms held her close. "I'll be ready by 5:00."

* * *

BY THE TIME Porter was due to pick up Emily, her hands were shaking. She felt like a teenager waiting for her prom date, shifting from foot to foot while hoping she wouldn't say anything too stupid. Except in this case, she was a full-grown adult, waiting for the man who made her grin from ear to ear.

There was a lot of pressure behind meeting a family. By the time Emily got to that point, she had usually been dating the guy for a while. The family didn't have to love her, but it sure made things easier if they did.

Emily had gone home to shower and get ready for dinner. Now she was back at the llama center dividing sensory toys into baskets for the therapists to keep in their rooms. She was pulling a tag off a pop toy when Porter's knock sounded at the door.

"Come in," she called, her heart lifting.

"How's my favorite person?" Porter asked. He lifted her hand and gave it a kiss before pulling her close for a hug.

"Pretty much the same as when you saw me a couple of hours ago."

Porter took an exaggerated sniff. "Except you smell much better."

Emily smacked his arm. "Hey, I put a lot of work into this look." She had debated back and forth between wearing her hair up or down, choosing in the end to do a combination of both. The hair along the front of her face was pulled back in a braid and the rest hung down in soft waves. It wasn't the first, or even second time she was going to meet Mom Matthews, but the pressure was on. Emily really wanted Porter's mom to like her.

"It's like I said before. I think you're beautiful no matter what."

"Thanks. You don't look too shabby yourself." Emily leaned into his side. She didn't think she'd ever get tired of hearing his compliments. Because of the way Porter treated her, she actually believed the words that came out of his mouth.

Emily followed Porter to his truck. He ran to her side and opened the door, but instead of moving away so she could climb in, he wrapped his arms around her and pulled her close for a hug. Emily leaned against his chest, enjoying the moment.

"What was that for?" Emily asked.

"I figure it may be my last chance for a hug before my family scares you away. I need to stock up."

He started to walk away but Emily grabbed his shirt and pulled him close. "One more for the road."

By the time they reached Porter's house, Emily's mind was spinning from all the information Porter had tried to teach her on the ten-minute drive. She climbed out of the truck, muttering facts under her breath.

Porter rested his hand on her shoulder and she looked up. "What if I forget something important?" she asked.

He laughed. "I'm from a big family. Of course you're going to forget something."

That wasn't reassuring. She held out her hand, putting a finger up for each fact. "You're in charge of the general management of the ranch. Thomas is over the animals, or he is until Hope comes back. Reid takes care of the planting, including your special heirloom tomatoes. And Bree's in high school." She stopped to take a breath. "Did I miss anything?"

"My mom?"

"Oh yeah. She's pretty much incredible and keeps you all in line. Oh. She loves to knit too." A funny thought crept into Emily's mind. "Has she ever chased you around the room with a wooden spoon?"

Porter looked at her, his eyes wide. "No way. We all knew to listen to her the first time she told us something. She never had to bring out the spoon."

"Somehow that doesn't surprise me. Okay. I've got them down." Emily allowed herself to feel proud. Keeping track of the three kids in her family was much easier than keeping track of the eight in Porter's.

"You got the half of us that are going to be there."

Emily's pulse was racing, but her mind was calming down. "Well, Hope is a senior in college, Hudson is off pretending to do college but you think he's secretly in the rodeo circuit, and the twins Finn and Wyatt are freshmen. Did I get everyone now?"

Porter gave her shoulder a gentle squeeze. "You're amazing. I'd be happy with you remembering our names. Now, can you promise me you'll relax and enjoy my mom's delicious cooking?"

Emily nodded. "If her cooking is as good as you say it is, I'm going to be fine." She took Porter's hand and followed him to the front door.

When Porter pushed open the door, Emily was anticipating the smell of an amazing home-cooked meal. Instead, they walked into a house filled with smoke, the alarm blaring as they stepped into the kitchen.

Porter's mom passed them with a large pot, dark smoke

trailing behind her as she ran to the back door where Reid was waiting. He flung the door open and she disappeared down the steps.

The smoke was making Emily sneeze. She bumped her hip against Porter's side. "Is this what dinner time usually looks like?"

Mom Matthews came back through the door, pulling large hotpads off her hands. She stuffed them in her front apron pocket and grinned. "Hi guys. Welcome to chaos."

Emily felt more at home in the smoky haze than she did at her own house. She smiled. "Do you need any help?"

Mom Matthews shook her head. "I've got it. Thanks though. We just aren't going to have any mashed potatoes with the chicken tonight."

Porter and Reid burst out laughing.

"How did you manage to burn potatoes?" Porter asked.

Mom Matthews pulled out one of the hot pads and swatted at him. "You hush," she said. She turned to Emily. "I'm glad you're here, even if it does smell like I tried to burn the house down."

Emily smiled. "You're fine. I wasn't expecting anything gourmet."

"I'm glad you understand." Mom Matthews placed her hands on her hips. She turned to Porter and Reid. "Alright, boys. Let's set the table. Hopefully the smoke smell will fade quickly." She started to open windows while Emily followed behind the men.

"Can I take something?" Emily asked.

Porter reached for glasses that were on a higher shelf

and handed her a stack. "You can take these and follow me," he said.

Emily held back a grin as she walked with him to the table, feeling relaxed. If this was the way Porter's family handled a mishap, she'd be fine. Some families she knew would be filled with anger at the situation, but Mom Matthews seemed to take it all in stride.

When the table was set, Porter showed Emily the large dinner bell that was hanging outside their back door. "This will summon anyone else who isn't here. Growing up we knew that if we missed the bell, we'd miss out on first dibs at dinner."

Emily pulled the string, sending the clapper clanging from side to side. "It's loud," she said.

"That's the idea. We can hear it if we're anywhere nearby. Of course, now we also use the modern form of a bell."

"Which is?"

"Our cell phones." Porter's laugh was easy. He had a relaxed air about him that Emily hadn't seen yet. Somehow, she found him even more endearing than before. He looked good, standing on the porch, with fields stretching behind him as far as the eye could see.

Emily wasn't sure what dinner with the rest of the family would be like, but she was eager to learn more about the people who helped shape Porter into the man he was. She grabbed his hand when he held it out and followed him back into the house.

By the time dinner was over, Emily's stomach ached

from laughing so much. The conversation around the table had been lively, but so had the energy. When Emily's family had dinner together, they laughed and talked. Porter's family did the same, with an occasional scuffle thrown in.

Reid had started one of the fights. Emily asked what it was like having Porter for a brother and Reid jumped up from the table. He ran out of the room and came back a few minutes later holding a folded-up piece of paper. One look at the paper had everyone around the table laughing. Porter lunged for his brother, pushing dishes out of the way, but Reid dodged his attempts to pin him down.

Mom Matthews cleared her throat and the men settled down, with Porter burying his face in his hands. "Don't do it," he said, his words muffled.

"You know I have to," Reid said. He unfolded the paper and handed it to Emily. Porter's name was written across the top, with large blocky letters.

Emily looked around the table, unsure what she was holding.

"It's his second-grade essay," Thomas said.

"Read it out loud," Bree said.

Porter lifted his head and shook it emphatically. "She really doesn't need to read it at all." He looked at Emily with wide, puppy-dog eyes, but it was too late.

"When I grow up," Emily began. She saw the next lines and began laughing so hard, tears ran down her cheeks. "When I grow up, I'm going to be president. Everyone will have to get two chickens and a cow and they will bring them to me so I can own the biggest ranch in the world."

She turned to face Porter. "Grand ambitions, much?"

"What can I say? I like my farm animals." Porter leaned back in his chair, folding his arms.

Emily kept reading. "I am also going to have all the airplanes so they can fly me to the moon and to the Grand Canyon."

"Please tell me you've taken him to the Grand Canyon by now," Emily said. She looked from face to face but the siblings were all laughing too hard to speak.

"Keep reading," Mom Matthews said, wiping her eyes.

"I am also going to own a dinosaur farm because people were mean to the dinosaurs and they made them all go extinct. And if my brothers take my toys again, I'm going to feed them to the biggest t-rex I can catch because my brothers aren't so good at sharing."

Porter raised his hands in the air. "That's it. I'm going out back to summon the t-rex right now. He pushed his chair back but Emily grabbed his arm, holding him in place.

Reid started a slow clap while he turned his attention to Emily. "That, my friend, is the guy you are hanging out with. You'd better not get on his bad side or you may find yourself dinner for the next dinosaur who wanders by."

Porter wrapped his arm around Emily's shoulders and leaned over to whisper in her ear. "Don't worry. I'll make sure to feed Reid to the t-rex before you."

As Emily leaned into Porter's embrace, she was surprised at how comfortable she felt. Usually meeting a family for the first time was awkward, but for Emily it was like coming home. She squeezed Porter's knee under the table.

"Thank you," she whispered. She couldn't wait to have Porter to herself so she could tell him just how much she enjoyed being there.

CHAPTER 19

Emily didn't realize that going to dinner with Porter would throw her into the world of the Matthews family completely. She naively thought that the meal they shared would lead to friendly hellos on the street as they passed. She didn't realize just how often they would be around.

Over the next couple weeks, she was constantly surrounded by Porter's siblings or Mom Matthews. Emily was setting up the printer when Thomas and Reid showed up on her doorstep saying they were there to work on the roof. She tried to shoo them away, insisting that she was fine getting ready for the center on her own, but they saw right through her facade.

"We report to our big brother. If he says we're going to fix the roof, we're going to fix it." Thomas tucked his thumbs into his belt loops. "Sorry, Ems."

Porter had spoken and the brothers weren't going to budge.

"I guess Porter and I will be having a conversation about that," Emily said.

"No problem. You can tell us what you discuss later. Now, which way to the ladders?" Thomas pushed his hand through his hair the same way Porter did, and Emily let out a frustrated huff. If they shared similar mannerisms, she guessed they shared similar stubborn traits as well.

"This way." Emily showed the men where her tool shed was and then headed back to the house.

She was reading an instruction manual while sitting on the floor, surrounded by desk parts, when Mom Matthews walked in. The smell of freshly baked bread caught Emily's attention.

"Sorry to barge in, dear, but I thought you could use a little snack." She held out a basket full of crescent rolls.

"You didn't have to do that," Emily said.

"Of course not. But Porter told us all about your llama center and I wanted to see it for myself. When does it open?"

Emily's heart surged with pride. "The ribbon cutting ceremony is three weeks away."

"And you're one of the therapists?" Mom Matthews set the basket down, producing a small paper plate from underneath the rolls.

The fresh baked smell was making Emily's mouth water. "Yep. I've also hired my friend Anna to work here. She is an amazing therapist who practices in Colorado but is ready for a change of scenery. Eventually we'll have four therapists rotating through the schedule."

"That's exciting. And who will take care of the llamas?"

Mom Matthews passed her a roll so large, it went to the edge of the plate.

Emily took a bite, chewing slowly to savor the homemade taste that couldn't be manufactured in a factory. "Anna is going to take care of the finances and scheduling and I'll take care of the animals. I'll probably have a lighter client load until we get established. It's going to be busy but I can't wait."

"I'm really impressed with what you've accomplished."

Emily's smile was genuine. "Thank you. I can't believe it is all coming together."

Mom Matthews set the rolls on a table near the door. "I'll get out of your hair now. I just wanted to check in."

"It was good to see you," Emily said. She waited until she could hear the car pulling away before she dropped all pretenses of manners and shoved huge bites into her mouth. Each bite was a taste of pure heaven.

Porter showed up an hour later. He pulled Emily into the first office and shut the door, wrapping his arms around her in a hug. When he kissed the top of her head, Emily melted against his body.

"How was your day?" She lay her head on his chest, feeling his warmth. He began to massage her back, each circle leaving tingles that danced through Emily's body.

"It's better now. Do you realize it has been five hours since I last saw you?" Porter wove his hands through her hair. "That is some sort of a tragedy."

Emily laughed. "I'm glad you survived." With Porter standing there, Emily was able to forget her frustrations with the Matthews family invasion.

Unfortunately, the irritation returned when he pushed back so he could look her in the eye. "Did my brothers get here?" he asked.

Emily scowled. "Yes, but I didn't ask for them to come."

Porter took a step back and shrugged. "I know. I figured you could use the extra hands."

"That's not the point." Frustration was clawing its way slowly up her chest, an angry monster that brewed beneath the surface, ready to pounce. "I told you I wanted to take care of things myself."

"Yeah, but I didn't think you were serious. I've seen your list. It's growing daily." Porter turned on his heels. He walked to her desk, pulled out the office chair, and sat down, his relaxed attitude a direct contrast to the storm that raged inside Emily.

"Why wouldn't I be serious about the work I'm doing?" Heat flashed through Emily's body. He wasn't just talking about her work ethic. He was criticizing her integrity.

The chair twisted back and forth, with an oblivious Porter in the seat. "I don't know. I guess sometimes you say one thing but it feels like you mean something else."

All of Emily's pent-up anger and frustration broke free. She held her finger up, shaking it at Porter. "Please tell me you are not serious. If I say I want to do things on my own, I mean it. How many times do I need to repeat myself before it will stick in that thick head of yours? If I want your help, I'll ask for it. In the meantime, I don't need you treating me like a baby."

Porter flinched back, bringing the chair's rocking motion to a stop. He watched Emily with a furrowed brow.

"Is that what you really think I do? You think I treat you like a child?"

"Well, what else would you call it? You have decided you know what's best for me and my llama center. I'm surprised you haven't started to tell me how to take care of the llamas yet." Her words were pouring out, a flood that didn't seem to have an end. Every bit of frustration flowed out, from the seeds of doubt planted by Gabe to every delay since. Emily had worked too hard to see her center fail, and the one person she thought she could count on was giving her no respect.

Porter pushed himself out of the chair and walked to the door. He paused with his hand on the handle, his eyes blazing with a fire of their own. "Fine. If you can't see that having extra hands is a good thing, we'll all get out of your way." He gave a curt nod and left the office.

Emily watched Porter leave, knowing she could run after him or beg him to come back but why should she? He was in the wrong. She had been handling things on her own for years. Gabe hadn't supported her idea of a llama sanctuary and Porter wasn't respecting her need to make it on her own.

She could hear her sister Kayla's voice telling her to stop being so stubborn. Her mom would remind her that sometimes it was okay to accept help. Even her grandpa would want her to calm down.

Fear, anger, frustration and loneliness fought their way through Emily's body. All she had wanted was support from someone, and now that she was getting it, she was in panic mode. She should run after Porter, but what would she say? Even if he came back, there was no way he was going to forgive her for an outburst like that. Once again, Emily's temper was ruining something good for her.

The sound of voices got louder as the brothers passed the house to get to their cars. It was her chance to apologize but her feet were frozen to the floor. If nothing else, the polite thing to do would be to thank them for their help. After all, it was Porter's fault they were at the ranch. Not theirs. Still, she couldn't move.

She stood, a statue of indecision, until the sound of their laughter and revving engines faded. Then she let out a guttural yell, letting tears wash down her face until she collapsed into the chair Porter had vacated moments before.

Was this what she really wanted? Opening the llama center was her dream, but did she really want to fulfill that dream alone? What was she trying to prove?

Emily leaned back in the office chair and closed her eyes. The house was now quiet, but instead of feeling peaceful, the silence felt heavy. She thought she wanted to be alone, but now the silence was so oppressive, it was difficult to breathe.

She knew where she needed to be. Emily headed out to the fields and whistled loudly. Wembley wandered over, the wool on his back all mussed up. He must have found an extra nice spot of grass to roll in.

Emily picked a few pieces of brush out of his wool before hugging his neck. "Well, friend. I messed up again. It's pretty bad this time."

Wembley stretched his neck to the ground, taking a

mouthful of grass. He didn't seem too worried about Emily's predicament but her stomach didn't unclench. She didn't know how to fix the problem she had created with Porter.

The llamas were great, but Emily needed a human perspective. She called her sister, expecting an outpouring of sympathy, but Kayla wasn't much help. Her shrieks were so loud over the phone, Emily was certain the neighbors could hear her.

"You did what?" Kayla yelled. "Did a llama kick you in the head and you lost your mind?"

The words stung. "I didn't call you for a lecture," Emily said.

"Maybe not, but you need one. He was clearly perfect for you, so why did you push him away?" Kayla was right, but her words did nothing to calm the storm inside Emily's heart.

"Ugh. Never mind. I'll figure it out on my own." Emily hung up the phone, feeling even more abandoned than before.

***

There was radio silence from Porter through the weekend. No goofy text messages. No calls to check on how she was doing. Nothing. The silence was far more uncomfortable than the help had been.

Emily's list of things to do was finally starting to lessen as she made progress through the tasks, but now working felt shallow. She was getting closer and closer to reaching her dreams, so why wasn't her heart into it? The truth was that she had gotten used to reporting to Porter. She missed filling him in on her day.

Even the arrival of her best friend didn't take away the hole in her heart. Anna was helping to hang paintings when she asked Emily about her mood.

"We're opening in two weeks and I feel like you'd rather be anywhere but here. What is going on?"

Emily straightened the painting of a giant yellow sunflower and stepped back. "I told you about Porter, right?"

"The name sounds familiar. Let me see. Is this the guy you've been telling me about every single day?" Anna scratched the underside of her chin. Then she bumped her hip against Emily's. "I know I was stuck in Colorado until yesterday, but yes, I remember all the things you told me about your cowboy. You have been talking about him non-stop."

"Well, I didn't tell you how I pushed him away." Saying the words reminded her how big the hole in her heart had gotten. "It was bad."

The floodgates opened and Emily told Anna about everything that had happened, along with why she was so frustrated. Anna listened like a good friend would, occasionally interrupting with a question but mostly just listening quietly.

Anna didn't have to say anything when Emily was done speaking. The look she gave her said it all. Emily knew she had messed up.

"Can I be perfectly blunt with you?" Anna asked.

"Go for it." Emily plopped down on the couch she had bought with Porter, another reminder of his presence in her life. A few days after buying the couch, Porter had shown up with an armful of throw pillows. He didn't think the couch would look right without them. Emily pressed a yellow pillow to her chest, bracing herself for a lecture.

"I think that for as much time as we spend sitting in our offices and helping people see a way through their problems, you've managed to put blinders on your own eyes. You've been hurt in the past. I mean, you know how I felt about Gabe from early on. He never seemed to be on your side. I think you're letting that past relationship with Gabe spoil your future chances with Porter."

"Don't you think I would like to leave all the scars from Gabe behind? It's not like I've pulled them out and am parading them around."

"No, but you're letting the scars from your past cast a shadow so long, it is blocking the light that the future could bring you."

Anna's words were profound. They hit Emily in the chest, right where she needed it. "I haven't thought of it that way, but you're absolutely right. I am so afraid of getting hurt, I'm not letting myself get in a position to be hurt at all."

"Exactly." Anna picked up another painting and held it against the wall.

Emily tilted her from head to the side, trying to assess if it was straight. She pointed her thumb to the left and Anna responded by shifting the painting over. "What am I supposed to do? I can recognize my defective thinking, but

I'm not sure how it helps with this situation. I've already stepped in a big pile of horse manure, so to speak. I'm not sure how to wash away that stink."

"Do you think Porter likes you?"

The little shiver of happiness that tickled Emily's skin when she imagined his arms around her was the only answer she needed. A man didn't hold a woman like that if he wasn't interested. "Yeah. I'm pretty sure he does."

"And you like him?"

"I'm crazy about him."

"Then we're going to put our minds together and figure out a solution for this mess. Honestly, I can't wait to meet your cowboy."

CHAPTER 20

"Why are women so confusing?" Porter asked, kicking his boot against a clod of dirt. "I mean, one minute she's laughing and hugging me. The next, she's angry that I offered to help her. I don't understand these creatures at all."

The cow that Porter was venting to didn't have much wisdom to impart. She watched him with large brown eyes, chewing her cud.

Her leg was healing nicely from the cut she had gotten a few weeks earlier. The skin had mended together without any need for antibiotics. Thomas was going to have to find another reason to call Hazel. Just thinking about his brother brought a new wave of frustration.

"So much for double dating. I mean, I can't even keep myself single dating." He leaned against the fence post and looked at the sky. Faint puffy clouds dotted the horizon, but above Porter's head it was clear. A few more weeks and the heat of the sun was going to make it uncomfortable to work outside.

He patted the cow's side, relieved she was doing so well. "Anyhow, thanks for listening."

Porter hopped on his four-wheeler and headed to the next field. He liked to circle the ranch to make sure they weren't missing anything important. A small problem one day could turn into a disaster the next if they didn't take care of it in time.

By the time he was done with his assessment, half the day was gone. It didn't help that Porter had spent a chunk of his morning talking to a cow. She was a great listener but she didn't have much to offer by way of advice. It was time to talk to a human.

Porter found Thomas in the workshop, hammering away at the bench he was building. His brother stopped when Porter approached and set his hammer down. "I know that look," Thomas said. "What's on your mind?"

Porter tilted his head back, leaning against the hard wall while he looked at the ceiling. He was trying to gather his thoughts. "Was I wrong in trying to help Emily?"

Thomas studied his hands for a moment. "I don't think so. I'm not sure why helping someone is ever bad."

"I agree. I know Dad taught us better than to leave someone floundering if you can see a need. Somehow, though, I've really messed up. I don't know what to do."

"Have you talked to her yet?"

That was the tricky part. The look on Emily's face made it very clear that she wanted nothing to do with Porter ever again. "No. After our argument on Friday, I'm not sure she wants to talk to me. I kind of got the impression she'd like to see me roasting on a spit over the fire."

Thomas smacked his brother in the shoulder. "Dramatic, much?"

"Hey. You didn't see her face. She was very clear that she doesn't want me anywhere around." Porter picked at a section of chipping paint.

"So, what are you going to do? You can't just leave her alone."

If Porter could answer that question, he'd be thrilled. "I guess I'll figure it out."

Thomas reached for his hammer but then he stopped. "Hey Port?"

"Yeah?"

"I just thought of something. Remember how Mom acted when Dad died?"

"Which part of it?" Porter's memories of the time were a tangled mess of him trying to deal with his own grief while taking care of everyone else.

"I'm talking about the food part. Remember how everyone kept bringing us dinner? That second week, mom snapped."

The event was seared in Porter's mind. He had opened the door to see Mrs. Johnson from up the road standing on the porch holding a casserole dish. "Mom," Porter had called. "Dinner is here."

Instead of walking to the door to greet Mrs. Johnson, Mom Matthews stood in the hallway and glared. "You take that casserole back and tell everyone else to stay away. I don't need your pity food." Then she turned on her heels and stormed back to the kitchen.

Porter apologized to a very confused Mrs. Johnson, thanking her for the food. He took the dish to the kitchen. There, he found his mom sitting on the floor by the stove, holding a dish rag in one hand while she sobbed.

"I couldn't understand why she was so upset about a dinner," Porter said.

Thomas nodded. "Remember her explanation later, after she had apologized to Mrs. Johnson? It wasn't the food that was the problem. It was her feeling like if she couldn't even feed her family, how was she going to be able to take care of everything else on her shoulders?"

Porter was starting to see the connection. "So, Emily getting upset about the roof might not have been about the roof at all."

Thomas nodded. "Exactly. I think if you can figure out what Emily is really upset about, you may be able to fix things with her." He clamped his hand down on Porter's shoulder. "And I really need you to fix things with Emily because she is good for you. It's been a long time since I've seen you this happy."

"Thanks for the advice, Thomas. I think you're totally right." He clasped his brother's arm before leaving. They had more than their fair share of disagreements, but Porter knew that if he was in trouble, his family would be by his side in an instant.

When Porter left the barn, his mind was racing but his heart was calm. He had an idea about what he could do.

* * *

THE REST of the afternoon had passed and all Porter had to show for it was a strawberry pie. He had spent an hour trying to make the crust right, throwing away the first batch that was too crumbly. Mom Matthews had offered to help, but Porter turned her away. "It's ironic to say this, but I really have to do this on my own."

She nodded and stepped to the side, working around him in the kitchen while she prepared dinner. She only raised her eyebrows once when Porter pulled out a special addition for the pie.

"Uh, Port? You sure you know what you're doing there?" Mom asked. She had paused mid-pour of her spaghetti sauce when Porter placed the item on top of the pie crust and began covering it with the chocolate cream cheese topping.

"Hey, I learned my cooking skills from you." Porter smoothed out the cream cheese and began to press fresh strawberries into the top. "Really, I'm hoping this will make her smile. It'll go with the note I'm writing."

"I'll leave you to it then."

Porter added strawberries until they were piled high above the crust. Then he melted chocolate chips and drizzled the chocolate back and forth over the top of the pie. He was making a mess on the counter but his mom still didn't say anything.

When the pie had set up, Porter carefully packaged it up in a box. He gave the pie a final check before closing the lid. If the pie tasted half as good as it looked, he'd be well on his way to wooing Emily back.

The hardest part was still to come. Porter sat at the table and began to write. He wasn't sure what words to use, but he knew he had one chance to get things right. He wrote and rewrote the words, scribbling them out and starting fresh until his thoughts began to flow. Then he grabbed a new piece of paper and wrote down what he was feeling.

Fifteen minutes later, Porter headed out to the truck. With his stomach in knots and his head pounding, Porter carefully set the pie box on the seat next to him. He had tied a red ribbon around the box and tucked the note under the ribbon so it wouldn't blow away.

The drive to Emily's ranch was the longest it had ever taken. Part way down the hill he realized Emily might actually be there, which brought on a new set of nerves. The words he wanted to say were written down so much better than words he'd have to fumble through. In the end, he crossed his fingers and prayed that she wouldn't be there. All he wanted to do was to drop the pie on the porch and leave.

When he got to the ranch, his stomach sank all the way down to his boots. Not only was Emily's truck parked front and center, there was another car parked alongside it. So much for no one being home.

Porter took a deep breath and eased his truck onto the driveway, letting it idle for a minute while he gathered his thoughts. He wasn't sure what to say to Emily if there were other people watching.

Finally, he reached for the door handle. He had many personality traits that needed work, but courage wasn't one of them. A man who could face his parents after letting his baby sister almost die was a man who could face an angry girlfriend. He pushed open the door and climbed out of the truck.

Walking up to the steps filled Porter's body with the jitters. There were a lot of memories tied up with Emily's ranch. The porch alone had changed a lot over the past couple of months as Emily had spruced it up, painting the door and adding a handrail. Their relationship had changed a lot as well. It reminded him just how much he missed Emily. He ached to hold her in his arms again and kiss her until she forgave him.

His heart was in his throat when Porter knocked on the door. He wasn't sure which would be harder. Emily opening the door and rejecting him all over again or Emily not being there at all. Porter said a quick prayer that Emily would be receptive to his apology. He was saying amen when the door swung open.

The person who opened the door had eyes similar to Emily's, but that was where the similarities stopped. This woman was closer to Porter's height, with short brown hair that curled around her face. She pressed her lips together, a small smirk trying to escape.

"Hi." Porter's brain was trying to accept that it was someone other than Emily who was answering the door. "Is, uh, Emily here?"

The woman smiled and held out her hand. "I'm Anna.

Emily isn't available at the moment. Is there something I can help you with?"

Porter shook her hand. "Porter Matthews. Can you give this to her?" He held out the box like a peace offering, and waited for Anna to take it.

"No problem. I'll tell her you stopped by." A smile danced on Anna's lips when she reached for the box.

There was an awkward pause before Porter remembered that he had done the job he came for. He thanked Anna and spun on his heels to leave, not relaxing until the truck door was shut behind him and he was safely behind the steering wheel.

It wasn't until the driveway had faded into the distance that Porter finally let out the breath he had been holding. Although he had prayed for Emily to not be home, he found himself pushing down the disappointment that she wasn't there.

She had woven herself into his life, and Porter wasn't sure what to do now that she was gone. He turned the radio off for the drive home and turned his thoughts to the Lord. If anyone was able to heal a relationship, it would be God.

"Dear Lord," he said, praying outloud. "I don't know a lot about too many things, but I do know how much Emily has come to mean to me. If it be thy will for us to be together, please work with both of our hearts so we can understand each other better."

Although no answer came, Porter could feel peace washing through his body when he drove up the hill to his house. He was going to trust in the Lord, no matter what Emily's response was, and let the Lord take control.

CHAPTER 21

*E*mily was washing a sticky glue off her hands when she thought she heard a knocking sound. She called out to Anna, but there was no response. When she came out of the bathroom, Anna was arranging a small selection of paper plates in one of the cupboards.

"Hey, are you sure we're going to need these?" Anna asked. "I thought we were using the kitchen for storage.

"Yeah, but you know we're going to end up needing a quick bite to eat between clients. Besides, if we have a selection of paper goods, we'll be prepared for the random treats I plan to bring in."

Anna shifted to the side and Emily caught sight of a square box tied with a pretty red ribbon sitting on the counter.

"Did you go shopping?" Emily asked. "I wasn't scrubbing my hands for that long."

Anna spun to face her. "I don't think you give Porter

enough credit," she said. "He's way hotter than you told me."

Emily was struggling to follow her train of thought. "I'm confused. What does Porter have to do with shopping?"

"I met him about two minutes ago when he dropped off this package for you." Anna set the paper bowls in the cupboard and pointed at the box. "He left a note."

"Did you read it?" Emily asked. She wouldn't be surprised if Anna had taken a peek. The thought of someone else seeing Porter's words first made her stomach clench.

"No way. But I can't wait to hear what it says."

Emily slid the letter from the box, her pulse racing. After days with no contact, Porter had come by and she had missed him by mere minutes. Did he smell as good as usual? Was he sporting his five o' clock shadow? Was his hair still incredibly soft? Most importantly, why hadn't he stayed to talk to her?

The letter was written on a plain piece of paper, her name written across the front with a strong cursive that didn't look anything like the blocky letters that second grade Porter used. Just knowing the letter was from him sent a shiver of delight through her body. She glanced at Anna, debating if she should move to somewhere private, but she knew she'd be showing it to her friend immediately afterwards anyway.

"You ready?" Emily asked.

Anna nodded. "I am, but it's not my letter. Are you ready?"

The thought crossed Emily's mind that the letter might not be good and her hands started to shake. "I want to open the box first."

She reached for the ribbon, untying it and setting it carefully to the side. Then she opened the lid. A gorgeous strawberry pie sat in the center, with strawberries mounded so high, they touched the lid of the box. Upon closer inspection, it was clear that the pie hadn't been made by a professional. The uneven crust wouldn't pass restaurant quality control and one side of the pie had way more chocolate drizzled across the top than the other side.

"Do you think he made it?" Anna asked.

"I don't know. I'd say his mom did but I feel like she'd know how to work the crust better. Maybe his little sister Bree helped."

"Either way, it looks delicious." Anna walked to the cupboard. "Are you ready to taste it?"

She was pulling down plates before Emily answered.

"You know I want to dig in, but I'd better read the letter first. I'm hoping the pie is a good indicator of his mood."

She unfolded the paper all the way and took a breath. "*Emily,*" she began. She looked up at Anna with doubt creeping into her voice. "He didn't start it with a dear."

"That's okay. A lot of people aren't that formal these days. Keep reading."

Emily took a breath and read the next line. "*I have been struggling to find the words to say to you all weekend. It doesn't matter where I am on the ranch. Everything makes me miss you.*"

Her eyes were starting to tear up. Porter's words

echoed her feelings. She kept reading. *"I'd like to say I understand what caused our fight last week, but the truth is, I don't really get it. My family was raised to always help our neighbors, but I can see that you were raised differently. Although I don't necessarily understand why the helping part is bad, I know that I hurt you, and I'm not okay with that."*

Emily held the letter to the side, looking at Anna's face. "Who writes like this?" she asked. "Have you ever met a guy who actually admits when he messes up?"

Anna's laughter filled the air. "Yes, I have. They're a rare breed though. Does he say anything about the pie?"

Emily waved the letter back and forth. "I have one more section to read."

"Well, what are you waiting for?"

"Okay, okay." Emily took another deep breath and began to read. *"I know I gave you reason to doubt me, but the truth is, my heart is in your hands. If you can find it in yourself to forgive me, please return my heart at your earliest convenience."*

Emily's brow creased. She looked at Anna. "What's that supposed to mean?"

"I have no idea. Keep reading." She gestured to the letter.

Emily read the final line. *"Porter."*

"That's it?" Anna asked.

"That's all there is. Not even a love or a sincerely. I don't get it." Emily silently re-read the letter, but the words didn't make any more sense the second time around. How was she supposed to return his heart?

After a moment she set the letter to the side. "Well, I'm

not sure what I'm supposed to do about the letter, but there is a pie that is calling my name."

Anna handed her two plates and a knife. "Let's dig in."

The knife slid smoothly through the strawberries until it hit the bottom of the pie plate. She cut the other side of the slice and slid it out, placing it on a plate for Anna. When she went to cut the second piece, she noticed something strange. There was a dark line running along the exposed edge of the chocolate cream.

"What on earth?" Emily asked. She poked the dark edge with her knife, and it slid back under the cream. There was clearly something in there. Emily started to laugh.

"What's so funny?" Anna asked.

Emily grabbed a fork off the counter and began to dig through the pie while Anna looked on. Anna placed a hand on her arm to stop her.

"You're ruining the pie," she said.

Emily ignored her friend. She could feel the object slipping out from under the fork's tines, so she dug a little deeper into the cream. "I've almost got it."

The fork slipped behind the edge of the object and she was finally able to pull it out. Butterflies danced through her body when she saw what it was.

"Do you see this?" she asked. She held the object out to Anna.

Nestled in her hand, covered with chocolate cream, was a copper heart. Emily took it to the sink to wash it off. As the cream washed down the drain, engraved details on the heart appeared. The name Porter was written across the front, with a cowboy boot next to the end of his name.

Emily began to laugh. "He gave me his heart. An actual heart. Where on earth did he get this?"

Anna peered over Emily's shoulder. "See this hole here? I'm guessing it is a Christmas ornament and he took out the ribbon."

Emily clutched the ornament close to her chest, her heart filling with hope for the first time in days. She leaned against the counter top. "He said I should return the heart if I was ready to forgive him."

"So, are you?" Anna came to stand by Emily's side.

Emily didn't need to think about her answer. "Absolutely. I know we have some things to work out, but I'd like to try to work them out with him."

***

EMILY WAS FINDING that the craft store in the middle of town was larger than the feed store. With the number of ranches nearby, she had figured the feed store would win by a long shot, but as she turned down yet another aisle filled with ribbon, Emily had to admit she was wrong.

She had tried to ask a clerk for help, but the lines were four to five people deep along every single register. So, instead of being a nuisance, Emily wandered.

Once she figured out that most of the aisles were labeled, Emily was able to move faster. She walked past dozens of rows of quilting fabric, appreciating the bright colors even while she realized she'd probably never pull her sewing machine out again. Understanding the basics of putting a quilt together did not create a love of quilting in her soul. She'd much rather be working outside.

Emily crossed through one of the long yarn aisles, marveling that anyone needed that many choices of colors. She walked past cross stitch threads and jeweled painting kits before passing through the baking aisles. Finally, she got to the side of the store that held beads.

A quick search of the aisle yielded a few bead designs that caught her attention, but they weren't quite what she was looking for. She found hearts of varying sizes but she wanted a charm that would represent her uniquely. With frustration mounting, Emily turned the corner. There, on the endcap at the very bottom, was the perfect charm.

Emily's heart was picking up speed as she drove back to the ranch. She rummaged through the tool box until she found a pair of needle-nosed pliers. With shaking hands, she pulled open a small metal ring and threaded it through the loop on Porter's ornament. Then she slid her charm on and pressed the ring closed.

She pulled out a small white gift bag and slid the ornament in. Then she covered it with a piece of red tissue paper.

Porter had gotten away with writing her a letter but Emily knew she needed to talk to him face to face if they were really going to resolve things. She climbed into her truck and turned the engine on, but her feet wouldn't move. If she was going to talk to Porter, she had to be absolutely certain that she was ready to accept all the parts of him, including his helpful family.

Emily pulled out her phone, fiddling with the case

while she decided who she needed to call for advice. Anna was obviously on Porter's side, and she figured Kayla would be too. When her phone slipped out of her hands, she realized who she really needed to talk to.

A quiet stillness filled the cab of the truck when Emily folded her arms and began to silently pray. *Lord, you know me pretty well. You know all the parts of me that are stubborn and all the pains I've experienced in my life so far. I'm sure you know Porter too. I'm about to head over to his house to try to make amends. It isn't fair for me to patch up our relationship if it is something I'm going to ruin a little later. If it is your will for me to pursue Porter, please let me feel some sort of peace. Amen.*

Emily kept her eyes closed until her breathing slowed down. A calm wave washed over her body, filling her heart with peace. When she opened her eyes, she was ready. She was going to trust the calm she felt and talk to Porter.

When she pulled away from the ranch, she noticed three of the llamas lined up along the fence, watching her leave. "Wish me luck," she said, but they didn't answer.

Emily's nerves were calm until she turned onto Old Ranch Road. Then her hands began to shake. By the time she pulled up to the large ranch house, her stomach was tied in knots. She knew the Lord approved her attempts to reconcile, but she wasn't sure if Porter still felt the same.

There was no backing down now. Emily raised her hand to knock, thinking through the words she wanted to say one final time. No one answered. Emily knocked again, turning her head to check the driveway behind her. It was then that she noticed a few of the cars were missing, including Porter's truck.

She took a cleansing breath of air, accepting the fact that no one was home. She was going to have to find her courage again tomorrow. In the meantime, she prayed that her courage wouldn't wander too far. She still had a gift to deliver.

CHAPTER 22

Porter was surrounded by towering trees and soft, green grass. He had delivered the pie to Emily many hours ago and she still hadn't responded. His heart was racing and his nerves were tense, but he had to be patient and wait for her answer. He was proving to be useless on the ranch so he'd gone to the one place he knew he could talk through his feelings.

The city cemetery had changed a lot since Porter buried his wife, daughter, and dad. He wove his way through rows of headstones until he came to the polished marker engraved with his dad's name, Branson Matthews. Porter sat on the grass so he was facing the headstone and poured his heart out. He told him all about Emily and his worries of dating seriously again.

Speaking the words out loud brought a deep pain to his heart. Somehow, in all the getting to know Emily parts of dating, he had forgotten that she would never get to meet his amazing dad. She'd never hear his deep laughter when someone cracked a joke, and she wouldn't see how hard he worked for everyone in the family.

The realization made his heart heavy but it also brought clarity. Emily was the woman he wanted by his side. She wouldn't ever meet his dad in this life, but she was the one he wanted to bring with him to visit the grave. His heart flooded with so much love for Emily, it brought tears to his eyes.

Porter's next stop was a little more difficult. He paused by a small headstone to brush his hand across the top of his daughter Claire's grave. If life had kept Claire alive, she'd be turning nine in a couple of months. He closed his eyes and let himself imagine what that would look like. In his mind, she would be a younger version of Bree.

Finally, Porter stood in front of Cassidy's headstone. He knelt on the ground and studied the marker that had her name written across the front, with a space to the side for his. There was no one else around when Porter closed his eyes and began to speak.

"Cass, I met someone. I think we both knew this day would come. You especially, because you've always been much smarter than me."

He could hear Cassidy's laughter in his mind. She had scored three points higher than him on the ACT in high school and that clenched her superiority.

"I wouldn't come here to talk to you about just any woman, but Emily is someone special. I trusted you with my heart many years ago, and now I'm ready to share that trust with someone else. I know you're up in heaven with a lot of jobs to do, but I wanted to let you know in case you've been watching over me."

Speaking the words out loud filled Porter's heart with a wave of peace. He opened his eyes and felt courage washing through his soul. Although part of his heart would always belong at the cemetery, he knew that he was ready to trust the rest of his heart with Emily. If she didn't answer him soon, he was going to show up on her doorstep and wait until she was ready to hear him out.

Porter stood, brushing small bits of grass off his pants. He rested his hand on the top of Cassidy's grave, saying goodbye. He knew he'd come back to visit many more times throughout his life, but he hoped that the next time he came, it would be to introduce Emily to Cassidy.

A slight breeze had picked up when Porter was leaving. He walked to where he parked his truck and turned back to face the graves. As he did so, a bright ray of light shot through the branches of the trees to illuminate a small vase of sunflowers. It was a clear sign from Cassidy that she and Claire were watching over him, and they approved of his actions.

With his heart feeling completely restored, Porter was able to turn his truck towards home. He was driving up the hill to the ranch when his truck began to make a loud clattering noise. The thumping intensified, followed by a loud screech.

Porter pulled as close to the ditch as possible, easing his truck out of the way of oncoming traffic. He turned off the ignition and popped the hood. Something was clearly very wrong. He needed to figure out what it was before the engine broke completely.

He was standing at the front of the truck, tightening a bolt that had jostled loose, when a car drove past, slowing to a stop. Porter looked up to wave to the neighbor but the hood was blocking his view. He was wiggling a pipe back and forth when someone cleared her throat.

Porter stepped to the side of the truck to see who was there. As he did so, tingles blasted through his body. Emily was standing by the door, her hands clasped together in front of her.

"Need a hand?" she asked. She opened her mouth to say more but Porter didn't give her a moment to speak. He covered the distance between them in a second and wrapped her in his arms, holding the future he wanted to have. When she didn't pull away, he began to rub gentle circles up and down her back.

"What are you doing in my neck of the woods?" Porter asked.

Emily tilted her face so she could look him in the eye. "I was hoping to find you at home."

Porter waved at the truck, chuckling softly under his breath. "Well, I almost made it. My truck had different plans."

"I can see that." Emily's voice was soft. "I'm glad I caught you." She stepped out of Porter's arms and he groaned. He had just gotten her back where he liked her to be. Then she turned to walk away.

Porter wasn't ready for her to leave. "Please stay," he

said. "I'll be done fixing the truck in just a minute and then we can talk."

Emily shook her head. "I'll be back. I need to get something from my car."

She walked back to her car and Porter took a minute to fasten the hose back on. He was slamming the hood shut when Emily came walking back towards him with a gift bag in her hands.

"Thank you for the pie," she said. "And thank you for the surprise." She clutched the bag close to her chest. "I thought about what you said and I have an answer for you."

There was a slight tremor in her hands when she handed the bag over to him. He pulled the red tissue paper out, tossing it onto the hood of his truck. Then he reached into the bag and pulled out the ornament he gave Emily. As he did so, he noticed a small addition jangling at the top. Emily had attached a small charm that hung from the ornament. His grin grew wide when he recognized what it was.

"A llama?" he asked. He turned the small copper llama over in his hands, admiring the way it fit perfectly with his ornament.

Emily nodded. "You said I could give you back your heart when I was ready to forgive you, and I am. I don't know where our future will take us, but I do know that we are worth fighting for. I want to spend time talking with you and finding a solution to our differences."

She stepped closer and closed her hand around Porter's.

"I also know that there is no way I'm giving you back your heart unless there is part of me attached."

His heart sped up when she rested her hand on his arm. "So, do you think maybe I can be a part of your heart from now on?"

Porter pulled Emily close, kissing her until they both were breathless. He leaned his forehead against hers, waiting until his pulse slowed. Then he wrapped his arms around her waist, waiting to speak until his voice was clear.

"I know I've overstepped and been in your way. I've even made things harder for you at times. I wish I could promise that I'd keep my big mouth shut from now on, and that I'll always listen to you. I don't know if I can do that though. What I can promise is that if you will be part of my life, I will protect you the best I know how."

Porter tucked the ornament into his shirt pocket after making sure the llama was still attached. He reached for Emily's hand and laced his fingers through hers. "Emily Hutchings," he said. "You make my world a better place. I love you."

Emily's face lit up with pure joy. Her voice was soft when she said the words he wanted to hear. "I love you, too."

There was no more need for words. Porter wrapped his arms around her waist and pulled her close, showing her just how much he cared. When they broke the kiss, he leaned against the truck.

"Thank you for rescuing me once again," he said.

Emily gave his hand a squeeze. "I always will."

***

A week and a half later, the Llama Center for Healing was finally opening the doors. Porter had promised to stay back and watch the progress unless Emily asked for his help. He was so glad he did. Instead of jumping in to solve every problem, he was able to work side by side with Emily. He saw her strength as she problem-solved to find creative solutions for even the most difficult of situations.

The day the center opened; Porter could hardly contain his excitement. It was a pleasure to stand in the front row and watch Emily as the mayor handed her a large pair of scissors. Wembley stood by her side, casually chewing on one of the ribbon ties that hung too close to his head. Porter was taking pictures non-stop when Emily cut through the giant red ribbon and tied it around Wembley's neck. The small crowd that was gathered let out a wild cheer.

Emily's eyes went straight to Porter's. He pressed his fingers together to form a heart before he blew her a kiss. When he added his claps to those of the crowd, his were the loudest of the cheers. Pride filled his heart that he was able to date such an incredible woman.

There was a small reception afterwards that went late into the evening. Porter stayed in the background, turning all the attention back to Emily whenever anyone commented on how impressive the center was. She deserved all the praise.

The crowd dissipated as the sun was setting, but Porter still hadn't gotten a moment alone with Emily. He waited until the final guest left before pulling her into her brand-new office. A large package wrapped in brown paper leaned against the wall.

Emily's eyes were tired but they lit up. "A present? For me?"

Porter nodded.

"Can I open it now?" she asked.

"I've been waiting all night for you to be free. If I have to wait much longer, I might go crazy. Then you'll be stuck with me on your couch as your first client."

Emily laughed. "I hope not. There are pretty strict rules about therapists dating their clients. I'd much rather see what you gave me." She tore the paper off the present and then stepped back, confusion written on her face.

"This looks familiar," she said. "Where did you take it?" She was holding a black and white photo of a cowboy looking out over a field. The hat was turned down so you couldn't see the cowboy's face.

Porter opened his phone and began to swipe through the screen. "There are many people who worked hard to get you to this place, but I think a lot of credit goes to one person who couldn't be here with us in person. He sent a little message for you."

Emily's eyes filled with tears as the video began to play. "Hey Emily," her grandpa said. "I can't begin to tell you how proud I am of you. I have watched you grow from a little girl to the amazing young woman you are today. I know you are going to help so many people with your center. I love you so much." Emily clutched her hands to her heart.

Porter leaned the photo against the wall. "This is a photo of your grandpa. I thought you might like the reminder of him in your office. He may not live close, but he is always thinking about you."

Emily reached for a tissue. "It is beautiful. How did you get that shot? I haven't seen it before in any of his albums."

Porter reached for his phone and swiped to the next screen while Emily dabbed at her eyes. He pulled up one more video. "I had a little help from Kayla. She has a message for you as well."

"Hey sis," Kayla said. "I am so excited for your grand opening. You know I'd be there if I didn't have finals in a week. I hope you know what an incredible example you are to me. You have shown me that it is possible to achieve any dreams I can think of. I'm so lucky to have you as my big sister."

Emily leaned against Porter's side. He wrapped his arms around her, pulling her close. "There's one more thing," he said.

"You've already done so much. I don't know if I can handle any more surprises."

Porter tucked a strand of hair behind Emily's ear. "This one is a repeat so it barely counts."

He pulled open one of the desk drawers and reached for the white bag Emily had given him. "I was hoping you'd keep this ornament at your office as a reminder that my heart will always belong to you."

The tears in Emily's eyes were all the confirmation he needed. Porter leaned down and sealed the deal with a kiss.

EPILOGUE - THREE MONTHS LATER

Porter stood outside the house, watching with mixed feelings as the tow truck pulled his white truck away. He waved goodbye as Emily held his other hand. "Are you sure you want to do this?" she asked.

Porter swallowed a lump in his throat when the truck turned the corner so he could no longer see it. He brought Emily's hand to his lips, kissing her fingers before he released her hand. The truck held a lifetime of memories, but he was making new ones with Emily every day.

"It's time." The truck hadn't quite recovered from stalling on the hill. No matter how many times Porter fiddled with the engine, it never ran the same as it had before. He was ready for a fresh start.

Emily wrapped her arm around his waist. He loved the way she fit next to him. "Thank you for being here with me." His voice caught in his throat.

"I've never been attached to a particular car, but I know

EPILOGUE - THREE MONTHS LATER

how much this truck means to you. It's seen you through a lot of good and bad times."

"It has."

Emily was good at letting Porter feel his emotions. He was going to miss the truck, but he loved what letting go of it represented. Letting go of the truck meant saying hello to the possibilities of a new future. He liked the idea of Emily being part of that future very much.

"Remind me what your favorite color is," he asked Emily, even though he knew the answer.

"Red," Emily said.

"That's what I thought." Porter led Emily to the back of the house, pausing before they turned the corner. "Remember the trust exercise we did at the tulip field?"

A smile crossed her lips. "I remember."

"Well, I'm going to need you to close your eyes. I have something to show you."

"No squishy caterpillars, right?" Emily teased.

"Not even one." Porter waited until Emily was ready and then he placed her hand on his arm. As they turned the corner, Porter's heart soared. He tapped Emily's hand.

"You can open your eyes now," he said.

A new red truck sat in the driveway, with a small trailer attached behind. "It's beautiful," Emily said. "Is that a strange thing to say about a truck? Either way, I think you're going to love it."

"I couldn't have picked it out without your help."

Porter pulled Emily forward. A faint shuffling sound grew louder the closer they got to the truck.

EPILOGUE - THREE MONTHS LATER

Emily's eyebrows shot up. "Is there something alive in there?"

He nodded. "You guys can come out now," he called.

Hazel and Thomas stepped out from behind the trailer.

"What are you guys doing here?" Emily asked.

Porter took Emily's hand, rubbing it gently. "I asked them for their help." He walked towards the back of the trailer, feeling suddenly unsure that Emily would appreciate his gift.

When he opened the latch and swung open the door, Emily's mouth dropped open. The trailer was filled with a thick layer of straw. Nestled in the middle of the trailer was a small tan llama with a red bow tied around her neck. Porter nudged Emily forward.

"Emily, I'd like you to meet Margo."

"Well, hello there, sweetheart," Emily said.

Porter's eyes began to water as he watched her step forward, her hand raised to meet the llama which was struggling to her feet. He joined Emily in the trailer.

"She's beautiful," Emily said. "Why is she here?"

Porter squeezed her shoulder. "I've been so impressed with how things are going at the llama center that I kind of brag about it a lot. I think some people," he nodded towards Thomas, "might be getting tired of it."

"Kind of tired?" Thomas said. "He won't shut up about you."

Emily laughed. "Sorry about that."

"Ahem." Porter cleared his throat. "As I was saying, I've been talking to lots of people about the good work you've been doing. Last week one of my friends called and told

EPILOGUE - THREE MONTHS LATER

me that he heard about a llama that needed a rescue center."

"Oh no," Emily said. "This is her, right? Is Margo okay?"

Hazel stepped to Emily's side. "You can't see it as well with the shadows of the trailer, but she's pretty malnourished. I kept her at the clinic for a few days to see if I could help her. Thankfully, she seems to be responding really well to the special diet I've been feeding her."

Emily reached for Porter's hand, her touch sending sparks through his body. "And you got her for me?"

Porter nodded. "I don't want to add to your burden, but I thought some of your younger clients might like to help take care of her. And if not, I'm more than prepared to make her the first official llama on the Matthews family ranch."

Emily didn't speak, but she held her hand out once more, letting out a small sigh while she rubbed Margo's cheeks.

"If it's okay with you, I'd love to keep her." Emily turned her head to face Porter and his heart exploded. She was looking at him with such joy that he wished he had brought her a dozen llamas.

"She's one lucky girl," Porter said.

* * *

Porter was leaning against the fence with Emily by his side. They had introduced Margo to the llamas a couple of days ago but Margo was incredibly shy. She was trying to graze but Wembley kept walking too close for her comfort. Finally, Porter decided to help her out.

He called Wembley, silently cheering when the llama immediately trotted over.

"He listens to you," Emily said.

"I mean, we kind of bonded when I babysat him." He grinned at Emily and then turned his attention back to the llama, reaching through the fence to pat Wembley's neck. Moments later, Emily scooted in so she could pet Wembley as well.

She nestled against Porter's side. "I never imagined my life would end up like this"

"Like what?"

"Well, I'm standing on a gorgeous ranch with my very own llama on one side of me and my very handsome cowboy on the other."

"Uh huh. It sounds ideal." Porter heard Emily's words, but he disagreed. He was the lucky one.

Emily squeezed his hand. "For the first time in my life, I finally feel like I have somewhere I truly belong. Thank you for being part of all of this."

Porter looked at the woman standing beside him, his heart soaring. "When I lost Cassidy, I thought I would never be happy again. You've taught me that no matter where life leads, the Lord has a plan for us. I'm so grateful that you are part of that plan."

"Me too."

The future was unclear, but Porter knew if the relationship with Emily kept progressing the way it had been, he'd be down on one knee before too long. Life had taught him

EPILOGUE - THREE MONTHS LATER

that time was precious, and he wanted to spend every minute of the time he had left with the woman beside him.

He brushed Emily's hair back, stroking the side of her cheek. With Emily by his side, the future looked bright.

* * *

Thanks for joining me on Porter and Emily's adventures. They will continue to make appearances through the Elk Mountain Series as their relationship grows. The family saga continues in A Checkup for the Cowboy.

ALSO BY RUTH PENDLETON

Rosecrown Ranch Series
Love at Rosecrown Ranch
Longing for Rosecrown Ranch
Leaving Rosecrown Ranch

Christmas Books
The Merry Mishap
The Santa Swap

Elk Mountain Ranch Series
A Llama for the Cowboy
A Checkup for the Cowboy
A Passing Grade for the Cowboy
A Secret Sunrise for the Cowgirl

Made in United States
Troutdale, OR
04/08/2024

19002828R10159